BEWARE OF THE MANOSAURS:
Half Men, Half Dinosaurs

Joan Brown

BALBOA.PRESS
A DIVISION OF HAY HOUSE

Balboa Press books may be ordered through booksellers or by contacting:

Balboa Press
A Division of Hay House
1663 Liberty Drive
Bloomington, IN 47403
www.balboapress.com
844-682-1282

Because of the dynamic nature of the Internet, any web addresses or links contained in
this book may have changed since publication and may no longer be valid. The views
expressed in this work are solely those of the author and do not necessarily reflect the views
of the publisher, and the publisher hereby disclaims any responsibility for them.

The author of this book does not dispense medical advice or prescribe the use of any technique as a form of
treatment for physical, emotional, or medical problems without the advice of a physician, either directly or
indirectly. The intent of the author is only to offer information of a general nature to help you in your quest
for emotional and spiritual well-being. In the event you use any of the information in this book for yourself,
which is your constitutional right, the author and the publisher assume no responsibility for your actions.

Any people depicted in stock imagery provided by Getty Images are models,
and such images are being used for illustrative purposes only.
Certain stock imagery © Getty Images.

Print information available on the last page.

ISBN: 978-1-9822-7524-2 (sc)
ISBN: 978-1-9822-7525-9 (e)

Balboa Press rev. date: 10/01/2021

Contents

Megasaurus
25 Feet tall

Frogasaurus, the 22 Feet tall, amphibious/reptilian, Manosaur,

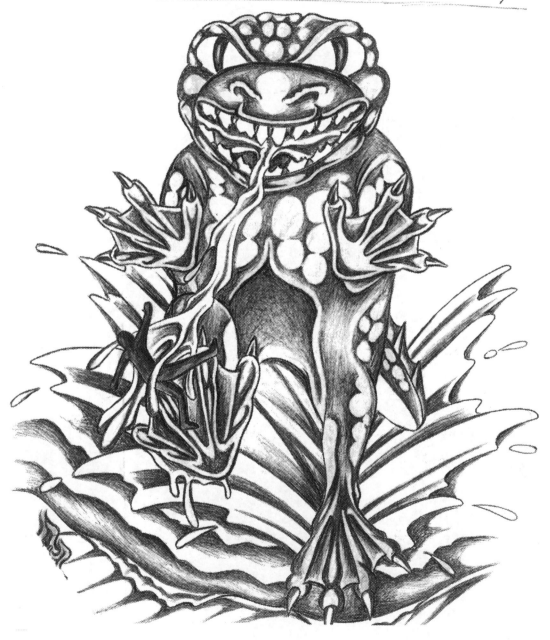

Tarantulasaurus, 22 feet tall,
Arachnid/reptilian, Manosaur

Draggonosaurus
23 Feet tall

Turtlesaurus, 20 Feet tall, Gigantic Biped Reptile

DEDICATION

Godmother of Paleontology

This book is dedicated to Mary Anning, the God-Mother of Paleontology. Mary is an unsung hero of science. Along the Southern coast of England, waves would crash against the sea cliffs. As the rocks eroded, fossils would be revealed that span into the Mesozoic Era, the time when the giant reptiles called dinosaurs lived. For centuries, local people roamed the beaches and cliffs searching for things to sell tourist and collectors. Although the labor was dangerous, Mary Anning's father taught her the trade when she was very young. After the death of her father, Mary used the strategy as away to help her struggling family. Anning was 12 years old when she found her first notable fossil, in 1812, which was the fossilized body matching the ichthyosaurus skull her older brother had found a year prior. Mary Anning soon discovered more fossils, including plesiosarus, fish, invertebrates and a pterosaur, Englands first.

Mary ended up opening a fossil shop. She was very intelligent and knowledgeable about anatomy. Mary died of cancer at the age of 47. She was honored by the Geological Society of London, and organization that did not admit women until our seventy years later in the early 1900's.

Also Mary Anning's finding entered museum collections under names of people who purchased them from her. Research based on her discoveries rarely acknowledge her contribution. She is the girl who sold sea shells by the seashore, but she also made a impact in science. This book is so many will always remember the name of Mary Anning. And God bless every child, man, and woman who are sick and fighting a cancer disease. A cure is on the way.

PROLOGUE

Mystical Prehistoric Fossils

The year was 1606 A.D.! Twenty poor people had formed an alliance, and joined together to dig for gold in Las Vegas, Nevada. Well at this present time it wasn't called Las Vegas. There was no state of Nevada; and the United States of America was not an independent nation with its own territory.

The uncivilized people lived poorly in tents. They had no guns to hunt with, no nice homes to live in, or no motor vehicles like we do today. None of those things were invented yet.

There was a thirty-year-old man by the name of Marvin Magalino. Marvin was a very tall and well-built man. He was very dominant and the most intellectual individual of the group of people. All twenty of the people gripped shovels digging their hardest in the field full of dirt. "You all need to dig harder! We've been digging for two days and we still haven't found any gold," shouted Marvin, seriously. "Son I don't think there is any gold down there", replied his father, Tyno.

Nobody else responded to Marvin, although their demeanor indicated the comment offended them. There were eight ladies and twelve men altogether, convinced that gold was within the perimeter of where they were digging. But Tyno was uncertain and skeptical. He was disappointed they had not found what they were searching for. Tyno and his best friend Timothy, were both 49 years old and were persuaded to accompany the group on the gold-digging expedition. The thought of being rich was a great temptation. It kept everyone optimistic and anticipating.

"Tyno, your son is over doing it. The sun is going down. We should just stop for today and resume tomorrow," said Timothy, exhausted.

Timothy was a strong man to be middle age. He was a few inches over 6 feet tall, and weighed 237 pounds.

"I do agree Timothy," replied Tyno, honestly. Timothy tossed his shovel in Marvin's direction. He was deliberately being defiant, and disregarding Marvin's instructions. Marvin glanced over in Timothy's direction losing concentration on his digging. "What is your problem Timothy? You are losing hope my friend," said Marvin, politely "No! I am not Marvin! I am just tired! I'm done digging for today," replied Timothy, tired. "Me too Marvin," said Philip.

When Philip said he was done, Marvin agreed it was sufficient for all the others to cease digging. Philip was a close friend of Marvin. The two had discovered the golden map together, and had decided to go dig for gold. They both practically shared the same determination and ambition of finding the valuable metallic elements.

"I guess you're right Philip! We should go ahead and wrap things up for today," said Marvin.

Marvin looked up in the sky and noticed the sun going down. Several of the other women continued digging a few yards away. A dirty blonde haired woman by the name of Stacey noticed a bunch of weird colorful fossils in the hole she was digging in. She started yelling to tell her colleagues informing them that she needed assistance.

"Marvin come here! I think I found something!" shouted Stacey, anxiously. The other men and women dropped their shovels, stopped their duties, and rushed over to where Stacey was. Stacey used her shovel to pick up over a dozen of the unusual fossils. She poured the dirty colorful fossils on top of the ground so everyone could see. Without hesitation each one of the gold-diggers rushed over to see the fossils and examine them. "These are probably old dinosaur fossils", said Tyno, the older man.

"How do you know Tyno? I've never seen fossils so colorful and weird looking before", said Timothy, curiously. "Neither have I. But those are definitely dinosaur bones in that hole down there. You don't see them" said Tyno, aware.

The other nineteen people were glancing down into the large hole. They saw three relatively oversized, unhuman bones. It was obvious the three bones were not from a normal animal. Half of the bones were still midway underneath dirt. But they were humongous. "No typical animal living on the land today, has bones that are that huge in their body," said Tyno, seriously. "I agree father! Those have to be dinosaur bones", said Marvin in agreement.

After looking down at the colorful fossils, a strange feeling started going through all of their bodies. The people started shaking like they were possessed by a powerful spirit, or simply having seizures. From a distance, Katy and Bryan could see huge dinosaur spirits entering their bodies. The couple stepped backwards away from the mysterious, and mystical transmogrification, occurring right before their eyes. They were the only two that did not touch the weird colorful looking fossils. Although they wanted to flee, they did not abandon their colleagues.

"Bryan what is happening to them?" asked Katy, astonished and worried. The couple stood side by side confused. "I don't know Katy! But I seen spirits of dinosaurs going into all of their bodies," said Bryan, afraid. "I did too," replied Katy. They both had clearly saw spirits of roaring dinosaurs, with huge sharp teeth, enter their friends' bodies. It was obvious their partners were now possessed with spirits of the ancient reptiles. Once the transformation was complete, the other 18 people looked normal. They all stood looking at one another curious as to what had just transpired.

"What just happened to us?" asked Timothy dumbfounded. "I have no idea, but I feel different," replied Tyno. "Me too father! I feel so much stronger," said Marvin. The pre-historic rocks, with dinosaur remains solified into them, were an unexplainable mystery. It was apparent the colorful fossils were possessed with some supernatural dinosaur spirits.

Katy and Bryan approached their gold-digging partners hesitantly. "Are you guy's alright?," asked Katy, concerned. Stacey looked into Katy's pretty brown eyes. "Yeah Katy. We're all alive, aren't we. We just feel unusual," said Stacey. As Katy looked into Stacey's brown eyes, she noticed a miraculous change in her eyeballs. Stacey no longer had normal human eyes. She now had eyes like a snake, alligator, or another reptilian. "Stacey your eye's look weird," said Katy, worried.

Immediately the others began examining one anothers eye's. It didn't take long for them to realize the tremendous change in their eyeballs. "Let's try and get those dinosaur bones out of there," said Tyno, seriously. Several men followed Tyno down into the hole, attempting to remove the gigantic dinosaur bones. The three huge bones from the ancient reptile was halfway buried in the dirt. Although they didn't know it yet, they were manosaurs now. As the men pulled the bones out of the ground, the ground caved in. All twenty of them fell 100 feet underground...............

CHAPTER 1

The Christmas Lights

"Mommy look at the house!," shouted Abagail, from the back seat. "I see it honey. Those are some beautiful Christmas lights. I like the way their family decorated their home," said Angel, her mother. Angel Nixon and her ten year old daughter were headed back home from the store. They had just finished Christmas shopping at Wal-Mart. As Angel cruised through the upper class neighborhoods of Las Vegas, Abagail continued making comments about all the pretty Christmas lights they passed by. It wasn't long before they arrived to their two story home. Angel parked the all-white Mercedes Benz, and exited out of the vehicle.

"Abbie grab some of those bags out of the back seat," said Angel. "Okay Mom," she replied. Abagail grabbed as many Wal-Mart bags as she could, and exited the back seat of the Benz. As she entered the house, her older brother Anthony came out to help his mother grab the rest of the bags out of the trunk. "Hey Mom," said Anthony, walking up to the Benz. Angel glanced up and replied, "Oh hi Son." "Need a hand," he said. "Sure! I can't toat all of these Christmas presents alone," she replied. The two of them gathered all of the bags at once. Closed the trunk, and headed in the house. "Mommy are you going to help me decorate the Christmas tree?" asked Abagail excitedly.

"Give me a minute sweetheart! We haven't even been home 30 seconds," replied her mother. The way her mother responded, made her a bit sad. "Alright mommy," she replied, sadly. Abagail sat down on the couch next to the Christmas

1

tree that was still in the box. Angel began taking the kitchen supplies, food, and other things out of the bags, and putting them away. "Oh yeah Mom! Florence called for you, while you were gone," said her son Anthony. "And what did she have to say?," asked Angel, carelessly. "Some new crazy story about those human dinosaurs. She's weird mom! I think she's on drugs or something," replied Anthony. "Jesus Christ!," blurted out Angel laughing. "It's not funny mom! I'm serious!," he replied. She continued laughing. "I know you are honey! But Florence is a very intelligent lady. She an Archaeologist son. Her job is studying ancient cultures as she digs up fossils, and old remains," said Angel, enlightening them. Anthony was 13 years old so he understood exactly what she meant. On the other hand, Abagail did not, and wasn't really concerned. All she was focused on was Christmas.

"I'm just going to go to my room! Take a bath and go to sleep. It 6:00 already!," shouted Abagail, upset. Abagail stood up and began stomping away to her room upstairs. "Be patient Abagail," shouted her mother. Abagail stopped at the middle of the stairs. She spoke softly and polite. She was tearful and seemed like she was going to cry. "But mommy you been saying that for 3 days now! We are never going to decorate the Christmas tree and put up the pretty Christmas lights like everybody else," she said, sadly.

Without further conversation, Abagail continued on to her room. Angel looked at her son Anthony. "Son finish putting these things away. I have to go up there and talk to your sister," she said. Anthony nodded at his mother and continued taking the food out of the grocery bags. He glanced up, and shook his head, as he watched his mother walk up the stairs to pamper his sister. Angel walked into Abagail's room. Her daughter was lying face down on the bed, with her face buried in the pillow. Angel sat on the edge of the bed, placed her hand on Abagail's back, and began rubbing it. "Abbie what's going on with you honey?," asked her mother.

Abagail sat up to speak to her mom. Her pillow was soaked with water and her eyes were wet. She wiped her eyes, leaned on her mother, and spoke. "Ever since dad and David died, you never spend time with me anymore; said Abagail sadly. Angel's emotions and way of thinking changed immediately. "Awww Abbie! I'm so sorry sweetheart." "I just miss dad and him so much." "Me too honey, I miss them too. Listen sweetheart. As a matter of fact, I think we need to go spend time together right now," said Angel. Abagail wiped her eyes again and eased up a little bit. Angel spoke again, knowing just what to say to make her little princess feel better. "I think we should go put up our Christmas lights. Then decorate our Christmas tree right after that," said Angel, enthusiastically. "Really!" shouted Abagail filled with excitement and happiness. "Yes baby. Let's go," said Abagail.

The mother had changed the topic, and removed her daughters focus off of the deaths. Abagail's dad and 6-year-old brother had died in a car accident a few months ago. Her dad was drinking and driving the night of the accident. Angel reminisced on the tragedy as she stood up. She was in the passenger seat and her 6-year-old son was in the back seat. The flashbacks were vivid memories, burned, and scarred in her brain. Fortunate to be alive, Angel tried not to recollect on the horrific event. After a few seconds pause and day dreaming, Abagail shouted. "Mom! What are you thinking about?" Come on!," said Abagail, readily. "Oh I'm sorry honey."

Abagail's voice brought her back to reality and the two of them walked out of the bedroom. They headed downstairs together and gathered the necessities to hang up their Christmas lights. "Anthony are you coming to help us hang up the Christmas lights?," asked Abagail, happily. "You better believe it," he replied, smiling. The three of them headed outside with the colorful lights, the ladder, the snowman's, the reindeers, the pictures of Santa Claus, and other things for their Christmas yard setting. The three of them laughed and made jokes together, as they set up the Christmas scene. They were united as a real family, like they hadn't been for awhile. Time kind of flew by quickly. It took them three hours to do the job. They weren't finished until 9:15 p.m. Although it seemed like ten minutes, they couldn't tell it took so long, due to the joy it brought to the three of them.

"Oh mommy we forgot to put the red nose on Rudolph!," shouted Abagail. She quickly grabbed the red nose, ran over and placed it on the lead reindeer. "Perfect!", said Abagail. "Anthony go turn the lights on so we can see how it looks," said Abagail impatiently. Angel stood directly behind her daughter, with her hands on Abagail's shoulders, awaiting for the lights to be turned on. As soon as he hit the lights, Anthony ran to the middle of the yard with his mother and sister.

"Wow!!! Our Christmas lights look cool," said Anthony, without thinking. Abagail said, owwwwuuuuu! He then said, "Yeah, our house is the shit!" Mom he just a bad word, said Abagail, her eyes getting big. "Anthony watch your mouth! What I tell you about cursing?," said the mother, upset. Anthony shrugged his shoulders and said, "Sorry mom!." Angel shook her head as she looked at Abagail. Abagail had her hand over her mouth, grinning. "Come on all of you. Let's head inside. It's getting late," said Angel.

The family departed the front yard and entered into their home. Abagail raced over to the Christmas tree to start decorating it. "Mom! Tell us at least one present you bought for us," said Anthony. "Okay-Okay. But I'm only telling you guys one," she said. "Me first Mommy! Me first," said Abagail, happily. "Alright girls first. Is that okay with you?," she asked her son. "Oh surrrrre! Why not?," he replied, sarcastically. "Jesus Christ! Okay here we go. Abbie one of these presents I bought you, was that 14 karat gold G. P. S. ring. So next time you get lost at Disney World, you won't be so hard to find," she said, smiling.

Abagail started laughing "I like that ring. Besides, running around Disney World by myself was fun, until these dudes started following me. That's when it got scary," she said seriously. "And my present," said Anthony, making himself known. "Anthony, one of the presents I got you was the new Genius phone," said Angel, smiling. "Really Mom!," said the young teenager, astonished, and surprised, by the news. "Yes Son. That is one of your Christmas presents," she said, honestly. "Aw man. Thanks mom! You're the best mom in the world," he said, seriously. All Angel could do was smile at the compliment. Angel loved her kids beyond dearly. She tried her best to make them happy, and keep the family close. Most of the initial pain of her losing her husband, and her youngest child had faded. She was no longer crying every night like she used to. Although she found herself looking at pictures of her husband, and 6-year-old son Andy, every night, tears weren't rolling down her cheeks as much.

"Alright kids! It's way past your guy's bedtime. I got a big job to do at the hospital tomorrow! And ya'll got big school work to do at school tomorrow," said Angel. "Alright Mommy, gimmie kiss," said Abagail. Her ten-year-old daughter ran over toward her, and hugged her mother. The two females kissed, and Abagail headed up the stairs to her room. "Anthony come give me a hug and kiss," said Angel, smiling. "Mommmm! Shouted the 13 year old. She knew Anthony hated the sentimental, mushy stuff. He wanted to be a big kid so bad. He didn't know once you get in the late twenties, you always want to go back to being a teenager again. He followed his mother instructions and came and gave her a hug. After the hug, she kissed him on the cheek and said, "I love you son," "Love you too Mom," replied Anthony.

Angel watched as her two children departed. She grabbed her cellular phone and looked at the screen. She had two missed calls from her friend Florence McKinley. "Oh Florence! You must of called while we were putting up Christmas lights," said Angel, whispering to herself. She tried calling Florence back. The phone went to the archaeologist voice mail. "She must be asleep by now," said Angel, talking to no one in particular. She stood up, off of the sofa, turned off the living room lights and headed up stairs to her bedroom.

CHAPTER 2

Hypothesis of an Archaeologist

They arrived at the capitol of Nevada, and exited their archaeology limo. Florence McKinley and her two male assistants walked inside the governor's office to meet with him. As she entered the office, she reached out and shook the governors hand. "It's a pleasure to meet with you Governor Kennedy," said Florence smiling. "Thank you Ms. McKinley! Please all of you have a seat, so we can discuss your proposal," said the governor. Florence and her two assistant's sat down in chairs. Florence sat directly across from the governor's desk, since she was the main speaker. The two men in black suits sat in chairs against the wall.

"Governor Kennedy, the A.E.F., which is Archaeology Exploration Foundation has sponsored my expedition. They have given me 10 million dollars to go down to Las Vegas to Las Ventures and explore. "Look at this," she said. Florence passed several pieces of papers over to the governor so he could examine them. She was quiet while Governor Kennedy overlooked the sponsorship papers. Once he glanced over them, he looked up at her. "And what exactly is it that you want me to do Florence?," he asked Florence looked at him and smiled. "Well Mr. Governor, The National Guards will not remove the steel barriers that block the passage way down into Las Ventures, without your approval. I want you to give them your authorization to allow me to go down to the underground city for 12 hours," she said, seriously. The Governor contemplated and thought carefully before speaking. "Florence I've heard the myths about the Manosaurs that so call exist down there. However, I do not believe such fairy tales and could care less, I was a business man before I was

7

the governor of Nevada, and I still am. So please, make me an offer! What will you pay me? If I authorize the National Guard Army to remove the steel barriers and let you enter down into Las Ventures," said the Governor smiling.

She looked in his eyes and spoke "Two million dollars," said Florence. "5 million dollars Florence. I want half," replied the governor. "Absolutely not! Three million," she replied "Four million dollars is my final negotiation and proposition," said Governor Kennedy. The 3 Archaeologist's looked at each other. The two men in the black suits nodded, at Florence. "Alright Mr. Governor! We have a deal! 4 million it is," replied Florence, smiling. She stood up and shook the Governor's hand. When are you planning to go down underneath Las Vegas?," asked the Governor. "Tomorrow morning! We'll be ready immediately," she replied. "Well Florence I will contact the National Guard today. I will have those steel barriers open for you at 8:00 in the morning. They will be closed right back immediately. When you are ready to exit from down there. Call me personally! I will have the guards reopen them, and elevate you up out of there alright," said the Governor. "Alright Mr. Governor! An I will have the money transferred to you in a few hours," replied Florence "Trust me Florence! I will get my money regardless," said Governor Kennedy, with authority.

Florence her two assistant Archaeologist departed the governor's office. They walked down the long steps of the capitol building. A long luxurious limousine was awaiting for the three. They entered inside the all-white, stretched out, Cadillac Escalade, closed the door, and the long limousine drove away.

⇨ The time was 4:00 p.m. when she arrived to her residence in Las Vegas. Florence went inside and got on her computer right away. She entered the precise information off the paper work, and transferred the four million dollars from her account, to the Governor's office. After she was finished, she began packing her Archaeology equipment. Florence packed her cameras, her magnifying glasses, and several other useful tools she would utilize, while down in Las Ventures. Florence took a deep breath as she was exhausted from all the movements of today's work. She sat down on her sofa, picked up her cellular phone, and decided to call Angel. The phone rang several times before Angel answered the phone.

"Hello" said Angel. "Hey, hope you're doing good," said Florence, happily. "Florence! How are you today?," asked Angel. "Great Angel! I have some good news," said Florence, excitedly. Angel became curious quickly from the way Florence made the statement. "What's the news Florence!?," asked Angel, quickly." The Governor

James Kennedy has given the authorization for me to enter Las Ventures tomorrow she said. "Are you serious?" That's unbelievable!" "Yeah! I know. I am going to find out the truth about Las Ventures." "Honestly Florence! I've done research. An come to find out those steel barriers have been there over 400 years," said Angel, informative. "No way! Then that would mean the steel barriers were there way before the United States of America was established!," she said surprised.

"Precisely Florence! So that brought me more suspicious, making me realize, those barriers are not American work. Upon further inspection, it's proving that steel the steel barriers may have been placed there from the inside," said Angel. "That may be correct! That is what has me so determined to know what's down there. Whoever put those steel barriers there, did it so no one else would enter or go down there," said Florence.

"I agree. And so far it has worked. Since our country has been established, no one has yet to remove those barriers, and drop down there," "Well Angel, tomorrow, Andrew, Ron, and I are going on a 12 hour exploration to see what's down there," said Florence, seriously. "I wish you luck on the expedition. I wish I could come, but I have an open heart surgery operation to do tomorrow," said Angel. "Alright Angel, I'll send you pictures while I'm down there," said Florence. "Please do so! I'll talk with you later." That was the end of their conversation, Angel hung up the phone.

December 6th 2025

Florence, Ron, and Andrew arrived to the steel barriers that lead down to Las Ventures, at 8:05 a.m. They were running a few minutes late. The 6 National Guard members were already there waiting on the three archaeologist to arrive. Florence, Ron, and Andrew exited the back seat of their business truck with all of their fancy, high priced, equipment. Each one of them had a backpack that obviously had their archaeology tools inside. The three of them walked over and approached the 6 National Guards.

"Ma'am you are Florence McKinley: Is this right!?," asked one of the chief guards. "Yep! That's me," she replied. "I will need to see your identification for verification," said the chief National Guard. Florence didn't hesitate to pull her identity necklace out. It was tucked in her shirt, between her nice sized breast. The men around her gave the well-groomed young lady their undivided attention. As she flashed the I.D., the chief guard stepped closer to her to examine it. "Alright Ms. McKinley! Thank you! Guards! Retract those steel barriers and lower these three individuals down into the underground," said the chief guard.

Without any discussion, the other 5 guards attached the heavy duty machinery to their barriers. It didn't take long for the guards to retract the gigantic old steel barriers. The barriers were hesitant to rewind. They had never been removed, or retracted since the day they were put in place. "Alright chief! The archaeologist can come on now," said one of the other National Guard members. The chief glanced over at the three archaeologist. "Alright you three! Head on over there and George into that portable elevator," said the chief guard. Thank you chief," said Andrew, politely.

Ron and Andrew both, were over 6 feet tall, blonde haired men. They both were fair looking men with blue eyes, and they both were attracted to Florence. Ron, Andrew and Florence walked over and entered the portable elevator with their belongings. Once they were inside, one guard yelled, "All aboard!" Once inside the guard closed it, another used his new technological machine and lowered the three intelligent archaeologist down into Las Ventures. In less than one minute, all three of them were 100 feet down into the underground city of Manosaurs. As they exited the machine controlled elevator, the elevator was quickly taken back up. Florence glanced up as the portable elevator disappeared above them. They heard a loud noise as the steel barriers were closing, and slammed shut. "Boom!" The barriers were sealed again, and the three archaeologist were now locked in the unknown land of the Manosaurs. Whenever they wanted to leave, all they had to do was hit their emergency button, or call for the chief to open the barriers and let them out, or simply call the governor.

"Wow! This place looks incredible," said Ron astounded. He was looking at the dinosaur habitats, and how they were so uniquely built. The dinosaur's homes, built by the Manosaurs, were quite different from the way normal humans built their residences. "I can't disagree with you Ron. This place is very architecturally designed. How could they be so intelligent?," said Andrew. Florence spoke up. "Because Andrew! They're just not dinosaurs! Don't forget they are half human. Who knows their I.Q. and intellectual status," replied Florence, seriously. "Yeah you're right. I wasn't thinking about that," said Andrew. "Well enough of the conversation. Let's start taking pictures and getting footage on the uniqueness of this place," said Florence.

The three archaeologist pulled out their camera's, and smart phones. As they began walking around, they continued taking pictures of everything they saw. They saw Manosaurs roaming around and recorded them. They caught a couple of them transforming and growing into their huge dinosaur form. They recorded what looked like a normal human, growing bigger, and changing into the ancient extinct reptile. "Oh my God! This is magnificent! This is marvelous! Ron take my phone and record me! I am about to go live on social media with, this info," said Florence, excitedly. Ron began recording her! Millions of people were watching as Florence McKinley went live on Facebook, being videotaped 100 feet underground.

"My name is Florence McKinley, and I am an archaeologist for those of you who do not know, Manosaurs are humans that are able to transform and take on dinosaur form. I notice their human bodies will automatically transform into a dinosaur form when they are extremely angry or hungry. These Manosaurs down here do not eat regular food or meals like typical humans. Many of them are herbivores, but some of them are carnivores. All of them most transform and eat an enormous amount of food to maintain. I've found evidence that these Manosaurs love living underground because of the moon, they automatically transform and go on a terrorizing rampage when they can look at the moon. Therefore living in Las Ventures is a safer environment for the Manosaurs and humans.

I really believe these creatures have been in existence for almost a thousand years now. Although many humans were indenial of these superior human dinosaurs, I am video tapping them right now as I speak, to prove they are alive, and living in today's world. Over two hundred of these Manosaurs reside right here underneath Las Vegas, in this underground city called Las Ventures. Honestly I believe some of the government knew these human dinosaurs were down here, cannot leave, or escape.

My theory is this ..... the government cannot detonate an explosive to eradicate, and wipe out all these Manosaurs, without harming the city of Las Vegas that sits right above it. Some species barricaded the Manosaurs inside Las Ventures a long time ago. Coincidentally, the gigantic steel barriers have kept the dominant human dinosaurs beneath us. I believe the government was probably left with one option, invade this underground city and try to kill off the Manosaurs with high powered artillery. The only problem is, they would never be able to tell the difference between a normal human and a Manosaur until the creature transforms. And by then, it would be too late.....

There may or may not be normal innocent human beings that live down here also, I cannot say. But my conclusion is this, Las Vegas accumulates billions and billions of dollars. Nothing is worth jeopardizing the gambling capitol of the United States. It would be kamikaze to wage war against the Manosaurs unless the military just comes down here and kills every"........ The recording was interrupted as one of her colleagues dropped the cell phone. The three archaeologist were attacked by two vicious reptiles. Although it wasn't caught on camera, the sounds of the dinosaurs screeching could be heard in the background.

It was no doubt, the two Manosaurs had devoured the three archaeologist, like they were breakfast of the day.

Florence, Ron, or Andrew did not bring any firearms down in Las Ventures with them. They weren't really equipped with any protection. However, even if they were, the pistols couldn't have saved their lives regardless........

CHAPTER 3

Invasion of Las Ventures

When Florence and her archaeologist partners came up missing and never made it out of Las Ventures, the president of the U.S. ordered the military to invade Las Ventures. The commander-in-chief gave the order, and the generals of the U.S. armed forces followed them immediately. They authorized and commanded 500 of their troops the invade Las Ventures, and eradicated all the Manosaurs. The soldiers were specifically ordered not to kill any normal human beings, or any people they thought were not affiliated with the creatures. However, they had no idea there were no normal people down in Las Ventures.

It was exactly 5:00 in the morning, and all was silent in Las Vegas. Most of the citizens were asleep when the military began to invade Las Ventures. The U.S. Army retracted the steel barriers so all the armed troops could enter the underground city. Once the barriers were open, 300 members of the armed forces were locked inside. They lowered the soldiers and artillery down 100 feet. All the troops carrying rifles with extended magazines attached underneath. "Close the barriers back!," shouted the lieutenant general. The general did this to prevent, and avoid, any of the Manosaurs from escaping during the invasion. The general had 200 more soldiers on standby in Las Vegas, just in case they needed more armed troops to assist the first 300. All of the troops, had body cameras attached to them. No doubt, the generals would watch the majority of the war with the Manosaurs from the military base in Northern Nevada. The high ranked superiors of the U.S. armed forces would he well aware of any deadly circumstances that the troops faced, while down in Las

Ventures. The generals departed Las Vegas, and headed toward their office base. The colonels, and all officials ranking underneath the colonel, remained above Las Ventures, to follow any orders given by the generals from the military base.

Once they were down in Las Ventures, the troops spreaded out in many different groups of twenty-five. They all went separate ways after awhile. Many of the troops were surprised at how normal and peaceful it seemed to be in Las Ventures. What they thought they were looking at was normal men, women and children. However, they had no clue all of them were Manosaurs. The Manosaurs pupils were like reptiles, if you could get close enough to examine their eyes. They came to exterminate them but they couldn't discern the differences from a normal man and a Manosaur. Other than their mysterious eyeballs, no one on earth would be able to verify a Manosaur, until the creature transformed, and revealed its true identity. The Manosaurs watched the troops closely as they walked through Las Ventures in their military uniforms, and assault rifles in possession. Tracey and her 6-year-old daughter Chyna, were standing outside their dinosaur habitat playing together. The mother and child glanced over and saw the U.S. army troops.

"Mommy who are those people?," asked the 6 year old girl. "I don't know baby. But I must go warn King Megasaurus at once," replied Tracey. The mother picked up her child and carried her away. "What do you think they are doing down here mommy?," asked Chyna. Although she knew exactly why the Army had come down to Las Ventures, she couldn't tell her baby they were out to kill them. "I don't know honey. I really don't know.," she replied, lying. The troops looked at the lady and little girl walking away quickly. The two were sadly mistaken for normal human beings. The troops didn't even think about shooting or killing the two. "All of these people down here seem like normal people to me," said Sergeant Matt.

"I agree Serg, but all of them are acting suspicious, like they have something to hide from us," said Hank. Hank and Serg Matt were best friends. They had been partners in the U.S. Army for over two decades. Sergeant Matt examined his next move. "I don't think their hiding anything! Their just afraid of us.," replied Sgt. Matt. Hank shouted "Afraid! We should be afraid! I saw the video of Florence McKinley and what she said. We were just lowered 100 feet underground into Lord knows what the hell this place is! And they're afraid! I seriously doubt that," said Hank worried.

"Chill out man, I don't think it's going to be nearly as bad as it was in Iraq," said the Sgt. walking with his machine gun. Hank was trembling. He was worried and was obvious he could sense a bad feeling. I am telling you Sgt. I got that gut feeling again. These people are in cahoots with each other. They live down here with these dinosaurs or Manosaurs, or whatever the hell you want to call them! Watch Serg! One wrong move and boom! The war is going to breakout and start! Just like in the movies," said Hank, afraid.

The troops continued walking through the underground city inspecting everyone with their rifle in hand. "Well this isn't a damn movie Hank! This is reality! There's probably three or four, maybe five or six dinosaurs down there. We're going to kill the damn reptiles and be out here before you know it," said Sergeant Matt, seriously. "You mean Manosaurs Serg. They're not simply dinosaurs," replied Hank. "Manosaurs, dinosaurs I don't give a damn!," shouted Sergeant Matt seriously. Several other armed troops started smiling, finding the comment humorous. The group of U.S. Army members continued moving toward the northwest of Las Ventures.

⇨Meanwhile, several Manosaurs were warning others about the armed troops that invaded. Brenda, Tracey, and her daughter Chyna rushed toward the northside of Las Ventures to King Megasaur's domain. The Megasaurs, Marcus, was the king and chief Manosaur. Many called him Megasaur for short. He was the first and only one of his kind. There were no other Megasaurs that existed in Las Venture. His deceased Father, Tyno, the Fyrannosaurs, mated with a Albinosaurs named Amilliyah, and she gave birth to Megasaur. He was a rare descendent of a Tyrannosaurs Rex, with different features.

Megasaur was the strongest Manosaur in Las Ventures. Although he was a carnivore and could be vicious, he was humble. Many herbivores and carnivores loved him and respected him with the upmost respect. The 25-foot-tall Megasaurs, sat in his gigantic chair watching his grandson devour his food. Megasaur, had slaughtered a huge Stegosaurus and had given the rest to little Rex to finish up. The 7-year-old, 8 feet tall Tyrannosaurus ripped the flesh from the dead Stegosaurus and gobbled it down.

"Little Rex! Hurry up! Finish the meal before your mother returns," shouted Megasaur. Megasaur didn't want his daughter Teresa the Trynnosaurus to come home and see Little Rex eating a huge meal. They didn't want the young Trynnosaurus to become obsessed with killing other Manosaurs and eating them. She was trying to teach self-control. Megasaurus got tired of watching the young Manosaur rip small chunks of the bloody food apart, and chew it up with his sharp pointed, amature teeth. "That kid is going to be a monster when he grows up," whispered Megasaur, to himself. The King of the Manosaurs, stood up off his throne, and came down.

"Alright Rex! Breakfast is over with," shouted Megasaur, seriously. The giant king stomped over to where the young Tyrannosaurus was, and snatched the blood remains with his gigantic jaws. Megasaur devoured the rest of the Stegosauru's within seconds. As he gobbled the food down, Little Rex spoke. "Pa-Pa I was going to eat all of that," said Little Rex sadly. It was obvious he was hurt that his grandfather had took the rest of the food away from him. "Listen Rex! Your mother will be home any minute now? She does not want me feeding you extra food behind her back lad," said Megasaurus, seriously. "But why Pa-Pa?," asked little Rex, innocently. The 25-foot-tall Megasaurus took a deep breath before he spoke. "Because little one. You are a special kind of Manosaur. There are not that many Tyrannosauruses left, and she wants to keep you safe," said Megasaur. "But what does that have to do with me eating food when I am hungry," he asked, confused.

"Rex, you can become addicted to feeding yourself. You could grow to be much bigger than I am, if you lose control, and start devouring everything you come in contact with. A Tyrannosaurus must control his eating habits at a young age or else... later, his eating will control him," said Megasaur, truthfully. Little Rex was silent for a moment. "I guess I understand," said little Rex, innocently. Megasaur didn't want his grandson to experience what he'd been through either. A Megasaurus was no different from a Tyrannosaurus. The two creatures were very similar to one another. Only difference was, the Megasaurus had longer arms, and a huge, sharp, curved horn going upward out of his forehead. Megasaurus's father Tyno was a Tyrannosaurus, and all of his past family were Tyrannosauruses also. It was Megasauru's mother that caused him to be a unique species. His mother bloodline was extremely rare. By her mating with the old King Tyno the Fyrannosaurs Marcus the first Megasaurus, came into existence.

After Megasaur was finished talking to his grandson, he transformed into Marcus, his human form. Right after that, Little Rex didn't hesitate to copy his Pa-Pa's actions Little Rex quickly began minimizing down to his 7-year-old human body. Megasaur and Little Rex spoke briefly about other concerns. It wasn't long before Rex's mother, Teresa returned to the gigantic domain. She entered the huge dinosaur residence with two other women. One of the female was holding her 6-year-old daughter in youthful arms. From their facial expressions, Marcus could tell something was amiss. It was very obvious by their body language, and intrusion, they were terrified and worried. Teresa spoke first. "Father! The humans are here to kill us!," shouted Teresa. "What are you talking about Teresa?," replied Marcus concerned. The lady holding the 6-year-old girl spoke up quickly, and answered before Teresa could. There are hundreds of humans with weapons to kill us, Megasaur! I know they have come to kill us all," said Tracey afraid. "Impossible! How did they get into Las Ventures?," he replied aggressively." "They came in through the steel barriers, and dropped down in here," said Teresa.

"Marcus took a deep breath as he contemplated. "I knew this day would come. The moment those humans moved here over 400 years ago; I knew they would become curious and get into our business down here one day. We been living down here in Las Ventures for centuries, and our ancestors lived down here for thousands of years. So if it comes down to it we must fight back," said Marcus seriously. "Marcus I am too old to be fighting against those humans with machines to kill us with," said Brenda, worried. Marcus looked at her. "I am too Brenda. I was born 1608. I am 417 years old. But I will not let those humans eradicate our species, disrespect our heritage, and ruin our ancient ancestry," said Marcus, upset. Little Rex could see the pain and discomfort in his grandfather's eye's and demeanor.

"Don't worry Grandpa I will help you fight," blurted out Little Rex. "I will help you fight those bad guys too. I'm not afraid to fight," said Chyna the 6-year-old girl. Tracey was still holding her 6-year-old daughter in her arms. Marcus walked over to one of the gigantic windows in the dome. The window was 20 feet wide on each side, making Marcus look tiny, because he was not in his Megasaurus form. He looked out the window and saw a group of armed U.S. military troops, a great distance away, Brenda spoke up and interrupted his thoughts.

"I believe in you Marcus. You are one of the strongest Manosaurs alive! You are the first and only Megasaurus in Las Ventures. Whether we win, lose, or die. I will fight beside you 100 percent," said Brenda, the older lady. "Thank you Brenda! I need a Brontosaurus by my side. You could help out alot," said Marcus, in his very deep voice. "Maybe we should set Tarantulasaurus and Draggonosaurus free! They could help us out alot with destroying those human's," said Tracey seriously. "Tarantulasaurus is dead," shouted Marcus, unware. There was a moment of silence, until Brenda spoke up. "Marcus, the Tarantulasaurus is not dead," she said, informative "What!," shouted Marcus, angrily. Hatred and fury filled his red reptile pupils, immediately. He walked toward his daughter Teresa to get close to her. "I ordered the raptors to put him to death, half a century ago, because of his rebellious and disobedient ways! Why isn't he dead?," shouted Marcus, hatefully. Teresa said, "They never executed him. They refused to follow through with it. They killed all the prisoners except him. Tarantulasaurus and Draggonosaurus are both still locked in Devil's Dungeon," said Teresa, honestly.

"And why didn't you tell me this long before now?," said Marcus. "Because father! It would have only caused another war. We have already lost all of our family of Tyrannosauruses in the last three wars. We can't stand another war father," said Teresa, seriously. "And all three of you women knew this and nobody ever told me anything," said Marcus. "Every Manosaur in Las Ventures knows they are alive Marcus," said Brenda seriously. Little Rex was very attentive. He listened carefully to their conversation. "Nope, nope, nope! Not me Pa-Pa! I didn't know about this," said little Rex, innocently. He was afraid of Marcus being mad with him too. "Father! Taran and Draggono have iron chains and chokers around their neck, ankles, waist and wrist! They cannot transform into their dinosaur form without committing suicide," said Teresa.

Marcus looked over at her in a mean way. "Don't ever keep a secret like that away from me! You hear me Teresa!," shouted Marcus. "Yes father," she replied, softly. Marcus inhaled and exhaled loudly. "I should of known better! Those raptors and pterodactyl's have always been beyond loyal to Tarantulasaurus and Draggonosaurus. Those two are like their guardian and kings," said Marcus. He paused for a second to think. "I hate to say it, but I will set Draggono free. He's my half-brother. It's the least I can do in a crisis like this. I can't leave him to die. If those humans are trying to kill us all. I might as well let the Draggonosaurus spit fireballs with pride. But I will not set Tarantulasaurus free! I hate that monster from the bottom of my heart," said Marcus, hatefully.

"Well we could use the help. Both of them are unique dinosaur's, and the last of their kind," said Tracey. "I wouldn't be surprised if the captor's and pterodactyls haven't taken the iron chain's and chokers off them already," said Brenda, plainly. "I doubt it! The raptor's and pterodactyls fear Megasaur. Besides, we have the keys to the Dungeon cells," said Teresa, quickly. "And what about Frogasaurus and Turtlesaurus? I haven't seen them in a long time. We could use their help too," said Tracey. It was obvious Tracey was sitting thinking of getting the 5 strongest and unique Manosaurs to come together, to defeat the humans with guns. Marcus looked at her and spoke. "I believe both of them are dead! I haven't seen or heard from Philip or Timothy in almost 50 years," said Marcus.

Extremely loud gunshots erupted from outside, interrupting their conversation. It was obvious from the rapid, repeated shots the military were starting to annihilate the Manosaurs. The four adults and the two young Manosaurs, rushed to nearby windows, to see what was going on outdoors. Several Manosaurs had transformed, took on their gigantic dinosaur form and attacked the armed U.S. military troops. There were 8 pterodactyls, 6 raptors, and 5 T-Rexs attacking the troops. The dinosaurs weren't bullet proof, but they sure as hell were taking alot of high powered bullets like they were.

The gigantic creatures would take over 50 shots to their body before even slowing down, or going down. By the time they were lying down on the ground, each Manosaur had already killed at least a dozen soldiers. As more Manosaurs saw what was happening, they transformed also and intervened. "Oh my God! The people are turning into dinosaurs," shouted a military troop scared. "I told you Serg! I told you Serg!," "Shut up and shoot," replied Sergeant Matt. As the military were shooting the huge creatures, loud roaring, screeching, and squealing, could be heard from miles away.

"Marcus we have to help them," shouted Brenda seriously. Without contemplating or procrastinating, Marcus began transforming into the 25 feet tall Megasaurus. Brenda transformed into the huge Brontosaurus, that was within her female human body. Her long neck was almost to the ceiling of the king's domain, and her immense long tail was just as lengthy. Tracey and her daughter transformed into the triceratops they were. Although the triceratops were shorter than the rest of the dinosaurs, they were very powerful and aggressive like a gigantic, snapping turtle. Teresa and her son Rex, transformed into their elite Tyrannosaurus form. "TERESA! Are you ready?," shouted Megasaur.

Teresa gave a loud roar that anyone could of heard miles away. "Let's show these humans that Manosaurs rule down here," shouted Brenda, the Brontoaurus. Without further elaboration, the 6 dinosaurs went charging out of the gigantic dome. Megasaur was leading the group with the others behind him. The 6 of them didn't hesitate to start attacking the armed military troops. Brenda was the first Manosaur to come in contact with the soldiers. While they were busy trying to shoot at the flying pterodactyl's in the air, the huge brontosaurus used her long tail and swept 14 troops off their feet. Some of them went flying into the air, dropping their rifles, and screaming from the impact. Many of them had broken legs. Some had broken limbs from the immense tail hitting their body, or the long hard fall back down to the ground.

Megasaur bent down low over 20 feet to the ground. He swiped both of his long claws across the ground to snatch up a group of troops. Although he was shot numerous times he grabbed approximately twenty armed soldiers. He had almost ten men in each hand. He held them up in front of him. The troops were petrified and filled with fear, as they looked in the eyes of the monster. Megasaur gave a loud roar sending wind, and saliva, flying all in the troops face. Afterward, he squeezed them; you could hear their bones cracking as he crushed them. Then he slung all of the men flying over 100 feet through the air.

It was inevitable the troops would either die, or suffer from a critical condition. Teresa, the mother Tyrannosaurus, and her young son little Rex, were attacking the troops with their vicious sharp teeth. They were eating the soldiers and crushing them with their powerful jaws. They were even stomping on some of the armed troops and kick the small people, compared to them. When they kicked the armed troops, many of them went flying through the air like baseballs.

The two triceratops, Chyna and her mother Tracey, were rushing towards every group of armed troops in sight. Both of the triceratops were charging the troops, trampling over them, and crushing them like they were insects. It didn't take the reptiles long to eradicate the small groups of military troops; although many troops were killed, 13 Manosaurs were dead along aside of the troops. 6 of the pterodactyls had been shot down out of the air by the machine guns, the troops were equipped with.

The 6 pterodactyls were lying dead, and so were 6 raptors. Teresa, the Fyrannosaurus was lying dead with many bullet holes in her. The other Manosaurs were all shot up, dripping blood, and injured badly. They looked over, and saw little Rex crying next to his mother. Little Rex obviously didn't understand his mother was dead.

"Mommy get up! Please Mommy get up. Don't go to sleep forever," said the 7 year old Manosaur, sadly. The young Manosaur brushed up against his mother very hard, trying to wake up his mother. Megasaur, Brenda, Tracey and Charlie were looking up at the 7 year old crying for his mother. "Megasaur go talk to him," said Brenda, softly. "I am Brenda. But all of us must remain in our dinosaur form else we might die from too much blood lost," said Megasaur; in a deep voice. The huge Megasaurus walked slowly to where his grandson, Little Rex, and his dead daughter Teresa, the Tyrannosaurus, were lying. Little Rex was still crying and talking to his mother.

"Don't die Mommy! No Mommy! Please Mommy please. Don't die on me on a day like this!," he said crying. The pain and agony caused Rex to become extremely weak. Within seconds he was shrinking down to his 7-year-old form again. The 25-foot-tall Megasaurus stood up behind the lad looking down at the sad Manosaur as he hugged Teresa and cried. Megasaur had seen so many casualties and deaths during the past wars of the Manosaurs. He had watched his father, his older brother, and many other T-Rex's die, during past wars. So Teresa's death didn't make him cry at all, or effort him emotionally. As he was looking down, he said, "Rex", in a very deep voice. The 7-year-old Manosaur was startled by the huge Megasaurus voice. He looked back, and looked up at the huge dinosaurs with watery eyes. "Yes - Pa-Pa," said the 7 year old Manosaur, hurt, lost, and worried. The little one was sad, and hiccupping. "Your mother is dead lad!," said Megasaur, roughly. "But Pa-Pa, I ..... I ...... I don't want her to die. I won't know what to do without her," said the young Manosaur, crying. "I know son. I know," replied Megasaur. The young dino looked back at his mother still crying from a distance. Megasaur shouted and called him to go. "Come on lad, I will have to take care of you from now on," said Megasaur, bravely. Little Rex looked at Megasaur walked to him and roared, and began transforming back into his dinosaur form. Megasaur walked over, and embraced the 7-year-old Manosaur. While embracing the young one, they heard numerous more gunshots that startled them. Megasaur looked up and shouted! "Manosaurs! More humans with machine guns are coming! We must go now!," shouted Megasaurus, seriously. The 5 dinosaurs began stomping away. Megasaur led the way, and the others followed them.

⇨The five Tyrannosauruses and the two pterodactyls rushed toward the middle margin. They knew leaving Las Ventures was the only way to survive. The five Tyrannosauruses were independent and renegades. They were not considered family or friends of Megasaur at all what so ever. Although no one really knew it. All 5 of them had full moon stones. Every Manosaur was under the impression there was only 5 stones. Honestly there was ten stones. The pink one, orange one, black one, brown one, and the purple one, had been buried with the rest of Master Mahatma's treasures, over a thousand years ago. All the Manosaurs knew the story of Master Mahatma and Lord Guru, but had no idea there were more stones. However, the Tyrannosauruses had found them, concealed them and on their way out of Las Ventures. Before any Manosaurs escaped, the five F-Rexs, and two pterodactyls, were the first ones to exit to the middle margin. Overall, there were still approximately 225 Manosaurs left.

⇨Rebel the raptor had eleven other raptors running behind him as he rushed into Devil's Dungeon. Not only were the raptors extremely vicious, but they were very quick also. Rebel was the leader and king of all the other raptors. He was 10 feet tall. Although he was short compared to the other Manosaurs, he was the tallest raptor and the biggest. All of the other raptors were between 7 and 8 feet tall. Tina the pterodactyl flew into the huge Dungeon right behind the raptors. Tina was a close friend of Rebel, and was like a daughter to the Draggonosaurus, and wanted to free Taran. She was in love with Tarantulasaurus. Only problem was she feared Megasaur and Tyrannosauruses.

Tina, Rebel, and eleven raptors raced toward the very back of Devils Dungeon to a steel barred cage. There was a huge cage with a human looking man inside of it. The man had thick, circular, iron chains and cuffs around his wrist, ankles, and waist. There was even a iron choker around his neck. The metal chains began jingling as he stood up in the cage. He could hear the dinosaurs charging his way, stomping and screeching. Rebel the raptor transformed down into his human form as he approached the cage. So did Tina the pterodactyl. The eleven raptors, behind them remained dinosaurs.

"Rebel! Tina!," shouted the man in the cage. "Draggono! The humans have invaded Las Ventures with machines to kill the Manosaurs!" said Rebel, seriously. "Please Rebel! Take these iron chains off of me! My Brother Megasaurus cannot leave me in here to die like this," shouted Draggono wickedly. "Listen Draggono! I haven't spoken to Megasaur. But me and my raptors will not leave you to be killed by humans like this," said Rebel.

He paused, and held up a huge gold key. "I will set you free under one condition!," "And what is that Rebel?," ask Draggono. "Swear loyalty and allegiance to me and all my raptors. That you will stand by our side and support us," said Rebel. "Haven't I always Rebel! I love you Raptors, even though you all have left me in these iron chains all of these years," he said. "Draggono you know we had no control over that! Megasaur put you in this dungeon and has possessed the keys for almost 50 years now. We went through hell to steal this one," said Rebel seriously.

"You have my word Rebel. But you all just don't betray me," replied Draggono. The vicious pterodactyl ran forward, transformed into her human form and stared at Draggono. His eyes became wide when he saw the female Manosaur. "Tina! My Child!," shouted Draggono.

"Draggono we never betrayed you! My mother was killed because of her love for you! When your brother Megasaur, teamed up with Frogasaurus to eradicate your dragons. All of the raptors fought beside me and Tarantulasaurus in the second war of Las Ventures. You knew fire breathing reptiles with wings was an abomination and against the covenant! You've been locked up in this dungeon almost 50 years. So you have no idea what we went through with Megasaur and his Tyrannosauruses. But we're still here to set you free again," said Tina, aggressively.

Draggono reminisced on the day he impregnated Saleena, Tina's mother. He knew by him being a Draggonosaurus, and her being a pterodactyl, they would create the flying breathing reptile, called a dragon. He wanted his own species, and legacy. Draggonosaurus did not have wings. Although he could spit fire balls. Huge fireballs. But he could not fly like a Dragon. The Dragon??? we're not only considered to be an abo???ation; and against the Manosaurs covenant. But they were ruthless flying - fire breathing reptiles. It was mandatory that Megasaur go and eradicate them. Besides he had promised his dead father that he would do it. Draggono spoke after reminiscing.

"I'm sorry Tina! I knew creating those dragons were against the covenant. I just want a second chance at freedom! I don't deserve to be in iron chains forever.," said Draggono, sincerely. Tina glanced over at Rebel. "Open the cage and set him free," said Tina. Rebel stepped forward, unlocked the gigantic cage, and went inside. He approached the Manosaur, inserted the key into various places and took off all the iron chains and chokers. The Manosaur smiled. "Thank you Rebel! Thank you Tina!," without any more conversation, Draggono began growing huge and transforming into the one and only Draggonosaurus there was. Since the raptors and pterodactyls were much shorter than the 23-foot dinosaur, they had to look up at him. His head was only 17 feet away from the roof of the caged dungeon. Draggonosaurus said, "Show me where Tarantulasaurus cage is located in this Dungeon," "Follow me!," said Rebel the raptor.

Rebel and all his vicious raptors took off running through the dungeon toward the location of Tarantulasaurus. Tina the pterodactyl flew right above them, and the huge Draggonosaurus followed right behind all of them. The human form of Tarantulasaurus woke up. He could hear the stampede of the huge dinosaurs coming his way in the dungeon. The pterodactyl was the first one to fly down and transform into a human. When the Tarantulasaurus saw her he yelled! "Tina! My Love!," Rebel the raptor ran over the dungeons floor to the cage and transformed into his human form quickly. The caged Manosaur saw Rebel and Draggono and shouted! "Rebel! Draggonosaurus!," shouted the man in the cage.

Everyone stopped and stepped aside and let the huge 23 foot tall Draggono walk up to the cage. The huge creature began shrinking down, back into his human form and walked closer to the cage." "Taran! How long has Megasaur had you in iron chains like this?," asked Draggono, sympathetically. "It seems like forever Draggono! How did you get free?," he asked curiously. "Rebel has stolen a key!," said Draggono. Taran looked down at them and spoke. "Rebel! I been nothing but good to your kind. When Draggono was thrown in this dungeon, I took care of all of your raptors. I protected you all from the Tyrannosauruses and Frogasauruses that would try to devour you all," said Taran. "We know Taran! But we can't set you free," said Rebel the raptor.

"What! Explain, why not!," shouted Taran, angrily. "Because we don't have the key to your steel cage," said Rebel "And why is that Rebel?," he asked, furious. "Because Megasaur keeps the keys to your cage. We managed to steal the keys to Draggono's cage, but Megasaur keeps your keys on him at all times," said Rebel the raptor. Taran glanced around upset. He looked at the iron chains on his wrist, ankles, and waist, and began yelling. Although he wanted to transform into the ferocious Tarantulasaurus he was, deep down inside, he could not. There was a solid tight iron plate around his neck. The iron plate would choke him to death before he even fully transformed into a Tarantulasaurus, if he tried. After he was done yelling, he looked at Rebel. "Where's that damn key!?," he asked. Rebel pulled out the key and tossed it into the cage. Taran picked up the key and tried to use it to remove the chains, and iron plates. When he realized the key was not a match to his incarceration, he threw it down. Rebel spoke. "Even if that key did take off your chains, there is a different key to open your cage Taran. Even the strongest Manosaur wouldn't be able to break this cage," said Rebel.

Draggono spoke up. "Taran you are my friend! I promise I will take those keys from Megasaur and come back for you," said Draggono, seriously. "Please Draggono! I been in here too long! I'm depending on you," said the Manosaur Taran. "We've been through alot together Taran. You can count on me to come back with the keys. Trust me!," said Draggono. With no further words Draggono began growing and turning into a dinosaur again. Once he fully evolved into the 23 foot Draggonosaurus, he turned around, and stomped away quickly. Rebel transformed into his raptor form, and Tina into a pterodactyl. The two followed behind Draggono, and the other 11 raptors followed behind, as they departed the dungeon. Tina said, "I love you Taran!"

CHAPTER 4

Frogasaurus and Turtlesaurus

⇨King Megasaur, Brenda the Brontosaurus, Chyna the 6-year-old Fricerotop, Tracey and 7-year-old Little Rex, continued their voyage toward Devil's Dungeon. They continued to fight and slaughter the U.S. Military as they came into battle's with them. The fully-automatic assault rifles were not an imminent death threat to the Manosaurs. The powerful gigantic creatures continued to crush the humans with their immense jaws and powerful legs.

Brenda the Brontosaurus, used her long tail to sweep the U.S. troops off their feet everytime. The armed soldiers would go flying through the air like a tennis racket hitting a bunch of tennis balls. The five Manosaurs were not alone in war. Other Manosaurs were transforming into their dinosaur's form and attacking also. Dozens of pterodactyls, and raptors were fighting back also. Some Manosaurs were getting killed after being shot a 100 times, and losing to much blood. However, more armed troops were getting killed than dinosaurs. A dinosaur would challenge the flying bullets and kill 12 to 15 troops before death. The Manosaurs didn't fear death or men. Many people they thought were humans were transforming into 20 foot tall, more or less dinosaurs. King Marcus, the Megasaurus, was destroying the armed troops. It was as if he was bullet proof. He was fearless! He had been shot over 90 times and still continued to slaughter the humans. Little Rex was just as vicious. It was plain to see why the Tyrannosaurus, and Megasaurus, were dominant Manosaurs in Las Venture.

⇨ "General! The soldiers can't tell who's who! No one can tell the difference from a normal human being from a Manosaur, until you're damn near ate by me," shouted the colonel. The Generals and high officials were watching the video footage from the body cameras of the soldiers. They noticed the suicidal destruction of not knowing a Manosaur from a normal human. The General picked up his radio and spoke with authority. "It's too risky! I command an extermination! Kill everything! I repeat! Kill everything!," shouted the Lieutenant General, seriously.

The sergeants and other leaders of the groups down in Las Ventures, heard the command. Honestly it was what they have been waiting for. Over two hindered of the U.S. armed troops had already been killed or ate by a Manosaur. Only approximately a quarter of the Manosaurs had been exterminated. The surprise attacks by the Manosaurs gave them the upper hand because looked like normal people. The general had given them authority to kill everything moving in Las Ventures. The Manosaurs would no longer be able to confuse or trick the troops.

"I order another two hundred men to go down there to assist the invasion! We are low on men down there. Those damn dinosaur humans are ripping my men apart," shouted the General, devastated without hesitation, the lower ranks followed the generals orders. They had the huge steel barriers re-opened, and began lowering hundreds of armed troops down in Las-Ventures again. Once the 200 troops were down in the underground city, the gigantic steel barriers were shut back.

⇨ "Megasaur we must keep moving! I am losing alot of bloody ground and blood," said Brenda the Brontosaurus. "I agree Brenda! The bullets are taking a great toll on me," said Megasaur's, seriously. "We must set Draggonosaurus free! The war will be much easier to win with him," said Brenda, seriously. Megasaurus nodded his head in agreement. He looked around for his grandson Little Rex. "Little Rex! Let's go," shouted Megasaur. Megasaur began stomping away. Brenda the Brontosaurus followed behind king of the Manosaurs. Tracey, Little Rex and little Chyna the triceratops did the same. They had no idea Draggono was already free.

⇨Devils Dungeon was many miles away on the west side of the underground city. Draggonosaurus and the raptors began slaughtering the armed troops violently and rapidly. Draggono was spitting gigantic balls of fire at the armed troops, eradicating them instantly. He was a unique dinosaur and very depraved. He was similar to a dragon, but had no wings.

Draggono never blew streams of fire out of his mouth either. He could just spit huge fire balls that would cause a blast of incendiarism. Many armed U.S. troops, retreated. They were reluctant to run out, and open fire on the 23 foot tall Manosaur. Rebel the Raptor and the other raptors loved Draggonosaurus. He made them feel safe and protected from any, and everything walking in Las Ventures. The raptors were the smallest of the dinosaurs. Draggonosaurus looked at Rebel.

"Rebel we must find Megasaur! I know he's not in his domain with all of this chaos going on," said Draggono, seriously "No! He's definitely out fighting against these humans. I bet you, we can find him and Teresa near the North bound area," replied Rebel, King of the raptors. "How sure are you Rebel?," asked Draggono. "Very sure! Those humans broke the steel barriers in South bound area and invaded us. Why would Megasaur in the others come towards the enemy with machines to kill us Manosaurs?," asked King Rebel. Draggono followed Rebels intuition and they headed north. Tina the pterodactyl and the other raptors continued moving behind Draggonosaurus as he lead the way.

⇨Philip, Timothy and Stoic lived on the East side of Las Ventures. They were very isolated from all the other Manosaurs to avoid altercations. Although Philip and Timothy were allies with King Megasaurus, over time their relationship became distant. The armed troops took awhile to arrive to the Eastside of Las-Ventures. The three Manosaurs were outside in their kingdom talking. Stoic was the King of Stegosauruses. Many of his species had been killed and ate by raptors, or another carnivore dinosaur. Philip and Timothy had been protecting the Stegosauruses to help their species reproduce. Stacey ran into the residence were the three male Manosaurs were gathered. They were startled as the pretty young lady entered the presence anxiously.

"King Stoic! The humans are here! They have crazy weapons and they are killing off the Manosaurs," shouted Stacey, terrified. "What!" Shouted Stoic, devastated by the news. Philip, Timothy and Stoic stood up quickly. "They are just killing us for no reason! They are hurting Manosaurs. Who are not even in dinosaur form," said Stacey afraid. "That means they have come to put a end to our species once and for all," said Timothy the Turtlesaurus. He was the last of his kind. No other Turtlesauruses existed in Las Ventures. "Then we must fight back. But if we can make it to the Middle Margin, we may be able to escape Las Ventures and go live in the real world," said Philip the Frogasuarus.

They all looked at Philip in a strange way. "Philip we will never survive in the real world. We are allergic to the moon, and we must transform to eat enough food," said

Stoic, seriously. Timothy spoke in agreement. "He's right Philip! Once they realize we are Manosaurs they will kill us with no remorse. Besides the middle margin exit, that leads to the real world, is 100 feet high. You are the only Manosaur that can jump up there," said Timothy. "If you all take on human form, I can hop all of us, right out of here," said Philip. They all were silent. "That's a good idea! But we don't even know if we will be able to make it to the Middle Margin," said Stoic. "Well I guess we have to go see just how strong these humans are with those guns," said Timothy, seriously. "Come on you all! Let's rock and roll," said Philip, readily.

The four Manosaurs began evolving into their dinosaur form. Stoic and Stacey began growing into the huge Stegosauruses they were. A double row of large boney plates grew on their spine's, as they evolved into Stegosauruses. Timothy fully transformed into a Turtlesaures, he stood 20 feet tall. Turtlesauruses was the fourth tallest Manosaur living in Las Ventures since Megasaurus was 25 feet tall, and Brenda the Brontosaurus was 28 feet tall. The Turtlesaurus was very unique. His shell was extremely powerful and tough; even a forceful fireball from the mouth of Draggonosaurus, could not penetrate, or damage his turtle shell. He had never been shot with a manmade firearm before, but he sure as hell wasn't afraid of bullets would harm him either. Philip transformed into the 22 feet tall Frogasaurus. The humongous green dinosaur was truly remarkable and one of a kind. Although he resembled the amphibian frog vertebrate, he was a dinosaur with huge pointed teeth. Frogasaurus belly was pure pale yellowish underneath, but the rest of his body was a greenish color. His four limbs were lengthy compared to other Manosaurs. Even when he dropped down on all four limbs like a frog, he was still extremely tall.

The four dinosaurs charged out King Stoic's kingdom for battle. Extremely loud, rapid gunfire, filled the environment of Las Ventures. They saw several other stegosauruses, triceratops and brontosauruses attacking the armed U.S. military troops. There were no pterodactyls, raptors, Tyrannosauruses or any other carnivores Manosaurs living on the East side of Las Venture. Majority of the carnivores resided on the west and Northside and the majority of the herbivores were united together on the east side, to avoid the predators. Frogasaurus begin snatching troops with his tongue and eating them. He was the only double-vore. He was a plant and flesh eating dinosaur. The stegosauruses, triceratops, and brontosaurus was getting slaughtered by the machine guns that the armed troops were firing. The herbivores weren't as quick and vicious as the raptors, tyrannosauruses, or pterodactyls.

However, Frogasaurus was very quick when he attacked. He was the quickest dinosaur roaming Las Ventures, excluding Tarantulasaurus who was chained in Devil's Dungeon. No dinosaur could move faster than the Tarantulasaurus. Philip the Frogasaurus leaped high in the air and landed on top of several troops crushing them instantly. Some troops managed to flee as they saw the gigantic dinosaur about to step on them. Philip transformed back into a human quickly. He picked up two machine guns, and began firing at the troops. He manage to dismantle a few armed troops. After one of the machine guns was empty, and out of bullets, he tossed it on the ground. He didn't hesitate to begin firing the other machine gun.

Philip was a ferocious Manosaur, and fearless. Once he sprayed all the bullets out of the high powered rifle, he threw the gun down, and transformed back into his dinosaur form. Meanwhile, Timothy the Turtlesaurus was moving recklessly, trampling over troops. He dropped down on all four limbs, and layed flat on the ground. After tucking his head and four limbs into his shell, he began spinning extremely fast. It was amazing how the gigantic turtle shell could move like a tornado running over the armed troops. Many troops began shooting at the spinning turtle shell, as it trampled over them. The machine gun bullets couldn't, and did not, damage the turtlesaurus at all whatsoever. The high velocity bullets repelled off the solid thick shell and the turtlesaurus ran the troops over. It was unquestionable if they survived being crushed by the thousands of pounds of pressure.

King Stoic, and Stacey used their long strong tails as their ultimate weapon. The two stegosaurus were shot numerous of times as they swept dozens of troops off their feet with their tails. The armed troops were flying into the air from the impact of the immense tails, as it crashed into their fragile bodies. It was inevitable. The military soldiers were either dead, or suffering from broken bones, disabling them from proceeding any further with the invasion. King Stoic, Stacey, Timothy and Philip manage to eradicate over a 100 armed troops with the help from other brontosauruses, stegosauruses, and triceratops.

As they wiped out the majority of the U.S. military that invaded the eastside of Las Ventures, they continued their journey toward the middle margin. They were nowhere near King Megasaur, Brenda, Tracey, Little Rex, and Chyna. The four Manosaurs were not concerned about the other Manosaurs at all. Their objective was to make it to the Middle Margin, and escape the invasion of Las Ventures. Although it wouldn't be easy living in the real world full of normal humans; they could take on human form, and be safer.

MAP OF LAS VENTURES

★ = Megasaur's Domain

XXX = Steel Barriers

Ⓓ = Devil's Dungeon

Ⓢ = Stoic's Kingdom and Stegosaurus' territory

Ⓡ = Raptor's Castle

Tri = Tricerotops Territory

F = Home of the old Frogasauruses

✳ = Tarantulasaurus old Castle

DGG = Draggonosaurus's old Lair

⠶ = huge trees

▲ = 50 Feet tall dinosaur habitats

M.M. = Middle Margin

Ⓑ = Brontosauruses Territory

Ptero = pterodactyls Cave

------- = the armed military troops trail...

✳ = Megasaur's current location

= Frogasaurus and Turtlesaurus's current location

Ⓧ = Draggonosaurus and Rebel's Current location

T = Home of the last few Tyrannosauruses that are left...

North

West

East

South

CHAPTER 5

Draggonosaurus Frees Tarantulasaurus

Draggono was the meanest Manosaur in Las Ventures. He was also the most feared. Draggono had a long body like a snake, the biggest claws, and the longest arms. The dinosaur had two long curved horns on his head like a ram. One on each side. Draggono, Tina, King Rebel and the other raptors moved quickly toward the north side of Las Ventures. It was only a matter of time before they would collide with King Megasaur, and the four dinosaurs accompanying him. It took awhile for them to run into each other, because Las Ventures was huge. The huge dinosaurs were moving fast as they took gigantic steps.

Ultimately the two individual groups of Manosaurs met face to face in the Northwest side of Las Ventures. They were near the huge pterodactyl cave when they saw each other. Neither party feared one another. As they approached each other they all came to a halt, a small distance away. Draggonosaurus spoke first.

"Well, well, well, King Megasaur! We finally meet again my brother," said Draggono, the Draggonosaurus. Megasaur looked into the red eyes of his half-brother. Draggono and Megasaur had the same mother, but different fathers. Although Marcus was hundreds of years older than Marcus, no one could tell. The Manosaurs never seemed to age physically, because they had a life span of a thousand years. "Draggono! I am glad to see you are already free. We were coming to set you free my brother," replied Megasaur. Out of disrespect, Draggono spit a small fireball on the ground. He was indicating Megasaur was lying out of his mouth. "Don't lie to me Megasaur! You have kept me locked in Devils Dungeon in iron chains for almost a half of a century," said Draggono, angrily. "Because you violated the covenant! You fornicated with Selena the Pterodactyl and created your own species of Dragons! And you knew fornicating with other species and mix breeding is an abomination," said King Megasaur, seriously. "How dare you Marcus! Me and you are both a mixed breed of species! So I can do whatever I want to do, to hell with you," said Draggono, angrily.

Megasaur reminisced on their parents and ancestry. Their mother was Queen Amilliyah the Albinosaurus. The Albinosaurus was a unknown and mysterious dinosaur species. None of the Manosaur's understood how she had come about, or ended up the way she was. Her blood line was one of a kind. However, Tyno the great Tyrannosaurus mated with her and gave birth to a unique son. Which was Marcus, the first Megasaur. Tyno and Amilliyah fell in love with one another. Their relationship came to a deadly end when the female Albinosaurus committed adultery, and became pregnant with a child from a different Manosaur. Rebel the Raptor knew the unborn child was his, but did not accept responsibility. He feared Tyno, the Tyrannosaurus Rex. Tyno had the beautiful Queen Albinosaurus killed for committing adultery, and becoming pregnant from another Manosaur, other than him. Tyno did not kill the unique baby, which was the unique Draggonosaurus. He placed the baby Manosaur near the forest by pterodactyls cave to die, or be raised by another species. Afterward, he told Megasaur to never let any manosaurs mix breed and create any superior dinosaurs again.

Megasaur stopped reminiscing and glanced at Rebel the Raptor. "So Rebel! Have you told Draggono the truth?" said Megasaur, seriously. The short, 10 foot tall dinosaur, became theatrically dumbfounded. "I don't know what you're talking about Megasaur," replied King Rebel, lying. Tina the Pterodactyl, and the other 11 raptors were attentive to the conversation. "So you have not told Draggono who his real father is. Tell him the truth Rebel! I know all about the abomination that forced my father to kill my mother," said Megasaur. Draggono looked at Rebel with his vicious red pupils. "What is he talking about Rebel?" asked Draggono. "Megasaur you are the Master of lies. You need an excuse for why you and Frogasaurus killed off the 5 dragons, and placed Draggono in prison for 5 decades!" shouted Rebel the Raptor, angrily.

Rapid gunshots began firing in their direction. Over fifty armed military troops opened fire at the 19 dinosaurs having a meeting. Without delay, Rebel and his eleven raptors attacked, Tina the Pterodactyl and Draggono attacked the troops. And King Megasaur, Tracey, Chyna, Brenda and little Rex attacked also. The machine guns were spraying bullets in every direction ripping through the skin of the gigantic reptiles. Although Megasaur and Brenda the Brontosaurus are elite, Draggosaurus was the most dominant dinosaur. He began spitting huge balls of fire at the armed troops and erasing them off the planet instantly. Two raptors screamed loudly, as they were killed by the machine guns. Although two raptors were killed, the rest manage to rip apart several military members. After the group of dinosaurs conquered the small group of militants, they resumed speaking. "Megasaur! Give me the keys to free Tarantulasaurus from Devil Dungeon!," shouted Draggono seriously. "No Draggono! He deserves to die! As long as you are free. That's all that matters," replied Megasaur, angrily.

Draggono rushed toward Megasaur and began fighting him. Draggo was too tired to keep spitting the huge fireballs, because it took alot of energy to do so. The other 17 manosaurs silently watched the two dominate dinosaurs fight it out. They did not intervene while the two half brothers fought aggressively. The Manosaurs were roaring and clawing each other very deeply, shedding one another's blood. Draggono was already tired from spitting so many huge fireballs at the troops, because it took so much energy. Draggono spit one minor fireball at Megasaur that hit him in the abdomen area. Megasaur fell forward down on all fours, like a lizard. The huge reptile raced forward, running like a lizard toward Draggono. The Megasaurus jumped up on two legs and slapped Draggono in the face, with his powerful claw.

Draggono gave off a loud roar as he clawed him back and bit Megasaur on the shoulder. The 128 foot Megasaurus was hurt by the bite. As Draggono released his bloody jaws, Megasaur pushed Draggono off of him. He then rammed the sharp long horn on his forehead into Draggono's chest. The fireball spitter stumbled backwards. Draggono gave off a loud roar again, and was angry by the sharp horn injecting in his chest. He then spit the biggest fireball he could at Megasaur. The Draggonosaurus used all his might to send the huge reddish yellow fireball, flying at Megasaurus chest. The fire ball struck the Megasaurus right in the chest, and sent him flying backwards about 10 feet. Megasaur was injured badly by the vicious incendiary dinosaur.

Draggonosaurus charged over towards Megasaur to finish him off. Megasaur laid on the ground in severe pain. Draggono stood over him and spoke before killing him. "I've been waiting a half century to do this to you Megasaur! You deserve to die my brother!," He paused for less than one second, then whispered "Long... Live...

King… Megasaur," said Draggono evily. Megasaur's eyes filled with fear as the incendiary dinosaur began to formulate a gigantic fireball in his mouth. Little Rex was scared as he watched. He shouted! "Pa-Pa! Get up Pa-Pa!"

Everything seemed to be slow motion for Little Rex. As Draggono opened his huge mouth to release the firey blast, Brenda the Brontosaurus swept Draggono off of his feet, with her long powerful tail. Draggono fell down on his back as the immense tail hit the back of his legs. Rebel and the nine raptors left, attacked the huge Brontosaurus immediately. Little Rex and Chyna the Triceratops, helped Brenda fight off the raptors right away. Tracey, the mother triceratops, rushed over to help Megasaur off the ground. "Megasaur grab my horns and help yourself get up," said the triceratops.

Megasaur grabbed the three horned-dinosaur and stood up off of the ground. Draggono stood up as Megasaur stood back up. Megasaur spit a huge key from up under his tongue toward Draggonosaurus. "Here! Take the key Draggono! But once this war is over! I promise you! I will kill that Tarantulasaurus myself when we meet again," said Megasaur, seriously. "Raptors! Grab the key and let's go," shouted Draggono, powerfully. Immediately the 10 raptors ceased their minor battle with Brenda, Rex and Chyna. Three raptors were triple teaming little Rex, two were double teaming Chyna and five were biting and ripping chunks off of Brenda. However, three bigger dinosaurs were elite compared to the raptors. Tina the Pterodactyl just observed. Rebel the Raptor grabbed the key off of the ground quickly. After a bunch of hateful eye contact, the raptors and Draggono departed. Tina the Pterodactyl silently flew behind the violent crew of Manosaurs. Tina loved Draggono, dearly. He was like her father figure. Draggono raised her and was practically her mother's husband before her mother was killed. She had no personal vendetta with Megasaur. Although he had exterminated the abominable dragon species, Megasaur was not responsible for her mother's death. The female Tyrannosaurus, Teresa, Megasaur's daughter had killed Selena.

Megasaur was in severe pain from the impact of the fireball hitting his chest. "Pa-Pa, are you okay?," asked little Rex, the 7 year old Tyrannosaurus. Megasaur looked down at his 8-foot-tall grandson. "Yes little Rex. I am alright," replied the 25 foot Megasaurus. "Megasaur we must leave Las Ventures! It's only a matter of time before the humans kill us all," said Tracey, worried. Megasaur was silent. He didn't really know what to say because he did not want to leave Las Ventures. It was his home. It was all he ever knew for the last seven hundred years. Brenda the Brontosaurus spoke up.

"Tracey's right Megasaur. They will continue to send more humans with machines until they kill us all. No Manosaur is safe down here in Las Ventures. We have a better chance of survival above ground in the real world," said Brenda, honestly. "I will not leave Las Ventures until Tarantulasaurus is dead Brenda! He killed my father and my brother Marvin. I cannot allow him to go unpunished," replied Megasaur angrily. Little Rex and Chyna the triceratops were listening carefully. Although they had no idea who Tarantulasaurus was, they could tell he was a violent rebellious Manosaur.

"Well we must at least get the kids to safety Megasaur. We are running out of time. The longer we wait, the more humans with weapons will come," said Brenda. "Come then! We shall get the children out of Las Ventures through the Middle Margin. Since the humans are invading through the steel barriers, the Middle Margin is the safest way to the real world," said Megasaur. "I'm just afraid of what it's going to be like up there," said Tracey, worried. "Me too Mommy! They're not going to like us up there," said Chyna. "Everything will be alright lad. Just stay out of the moonlight at night; And when you eat, don't let the humans see you turn into a dinosaur," said Megasaur, seriously. "Those are the two hardest things Megasaur," said Brenda, the Brontosaurus. "It's not difficult to do Brenda! It's the only way you all are going to survive up there. We are half human and we never grow old. We will fit in with them. If someone realizes you are a Manosaur, just run and leave that city," said Megasaur, informative.

"It's easy for you to say, when you have a full moon stone Megasaur," said Brenda. Megasaur did not reply to the comment. He changed the topic instead. "Let's go to the Middle Margin and get the young Manosaurs out of here," said Megasaur. As the monstrous Megasaurus roared, and began stomping away, the others followed him. The five dinosaurs stomped away toward the Middle Margin quickly. They were not far from their destination. They were presently located near Pterodactyls cave, which was only a few miles away from the Margin. "Surely it would take enormous creatures less than ten minutes to get there."

⇨ Meanwhile Draggonosaurus and the raptors were entering back into Devils Dungeon to free Tarantulasaurus. Although Draggono was anxious to question Rebel about Megasaur's allegations, he decided to wait to a later time. The 12 dinosaurs moved quickly through the dungeon, toward Taran's location. It was getting late towards the evening time. The war in Las Ventures had been going on for 13 hours now. The troops had invaded the underground very early that morning and it was well past 6:00 p.m. now. Taran was sleeping in his cell when he heard the loud footsteps of what he knew was manosaurs. He quickly jolted out of the bed and rushed the iron bars. When he saw Tiny, Rebel, and Draggono he smiled.

"Draggono! I knew you would come back for me my friend," said Taran, Rebel transformed down to his human form; Afterward, Tina and Draggono did the same. "I would never forsake you Taran! Every time I went to war and needed your help, you were there by my side," replied Draggono. Rebel handed the key to Draggono. He stepped forward, unlocked the metal bars, and walked inside. Taran looked at him and spoke. "And anytime you need me from this day forward I will still be by your side," said Taran, seriously. Draggono smiled as he began unlocking and removing the iron chains off of Taran. Once all of the iron plates and metal braces were removed from his neck, waist and ankles, he shook Draggono's hand. "Thank you Draggono. It's been 48 years of misery since Megasaur placed me in this dungeon," said Taran, relieved.

"I feel your pain. I am 70 years old now! That monster had me chained down for 5 decades! If it wasn't for Rebel stealing the key, neither one of us would be free right now," said Draggono. Taran looked at Rebel and said; "Thanks Rebel. You and your raptors have always shown great love and loyalty to me and my pterodactyls. I just wish someone would of came get me before now. But Megasaur will pay for this pain and agony he has caused me. I will send him straight to hell with his brother and father," said Taran angrily. Tina walked up to him the love of her life and looked in his eyes. "I'm sorry Taran," she said, sadly.

He replied angrily. "You should be Tina! I loved you and your pterodactyls like you were my family. And none of you had the audacity to find a way to set me free," said Taran, mad. "It's not our fault Tarantulasaurus! You know none of the pterodactyls are physically strong enough to challenge Megasaurus. With you and Draggono imprisoned, Marcus was unstoppable, and you know it Taran," shouted Tina. Draggono intervened. "She's right Taran. Megasaur and his Tyrannosauruses would devour anything in Las Ventures. You and I were the only threat of rebellion," said Draggono, truthful.

"No Draggono! You were placed in chains 2 years before I was. I eradicated almost all of those Tyrannosauruses one by one. Once Tyno and Marvin were dead, the rest of the Tyrannosauruses were easy to kill. There should only be a few Tyrannosauruses left living. That's Teresa, and the 5 renegades. Megasaur has done a great job of keeping himself and Teresa alive. If it wasn't for Turtlesaurus and Frogasaurus helping put me in this dungeon, we would all be ruling Las Ventures," said Taran upset. "Well, we all must evacuate Las Ventures! The humans have come down through the steel barriers with machines and are killing us all," said Rebel the Raptor. "What! Impossible," shouted Taran. Although Taran was angry, he could control his transformation. Anger was not a force that dictated, or triggered him to change into his dinosaur form. "Yes, it's very possible. They have been killing us all for hours now! We've been at war with them for more than a half a day now," said Rebel.

"Well then! We'll just have to kill them off as they come," said Taran. Draggono said, "No Taran. It will not work. You've been in this dungeon! You have to go out there and see it for yourself. The humans have machines that never stops killing. Or it seems that way. And they will only keep sending more humans, with more weapons, until we are all dead! We must leave Las Ventures and go up into the real world," said Draggono, truthfully. Taran was silent as he looked around contemplating. "We will not live long up there. The humans will kill us as soon as they realize we are elite and superior over them. We need full moon stones to live normal up there," said Taran. "I agree," said Draggono "Wait- Wait! Full moon stones! What is that?," asked Tina, curiously. Rebel pulled out a red full moon stone, and held it up in his hand.

"This is a full moon stone", he said. "Where did you get that from?," asked Taran excited. "I've had one for over a half century! I stole it from Frogasaurus. I know that slimey green manosaur has two more? There's only 5 full moon stones that exist! I know Turtlesaurus has the yellow one! And Megasaurus has the powerful gray one that was passed on to him from his father Tyno," said Taran. "Yes - Yes! But Frogasaurus still has the blue one and green one," said Rebel. "Then we must kill Frogasaurus and Turtlesaurus! We need those two full moon stones to live normal in the real world," said Taran. Tina interrupted, "Would someone please tell me what's so special about the damn stone!," shouted Tina, curiously. Draggono looked at Tina and spoke first. "The full moon stones are what we need to be normal like humans. It gives us the power to roam at night under the moon without being forced into a violent dinosaur by the moon light. It also keeps us full. We don't have to transform and eat every day because the stone absorbs minerals from the sun and moon that feeds the Manosaur," said Draggono. "Are you serious?," asked Tina.

Rebel said "He's very serious. With this full moon stone. I can remain normal as long as I want, and go days without eating," The group of Manosaur's were interrupted by the sound of machine guns outside of the dungeon. Then quickly repeated gunshots startled all of them. "The humans are here! We must go! We have to get to the Middle Margin and leave Las Ventures," shouted Draggono, seriously. The four Manosaurs who were in their human form did not hesitate to transform into their dinosaur form. Tina turned into the biggest pterodactyl in Las Ventures like she was. Rebel began transforming into the 10 foot tall, King Raptor he was.

Draggono began growing immense, into the 23-foot-tall, fireball spitting dinosaur. Draggono was not as huge as the Tarantulasaurus that was growing in front of him. Although the Tarantulasaurus was only 2 foot taller than Draggono, he was bigger. The creature was the only dinosaur with 8 limbs. The Tarantulasaurus stood tall on four legs like a Brontosaurus. Except he didn't have a long neck. He had a huge, long, upper body like a Tyrannosaurus, and four long arms. Tarantulasaurus was the most feared Manosaur because of his spider web. The black dinosaur could spray strings of long sticky web. The web came out of his tail and out of his mouth causing his adversaries a very sticky problem! Not only that.

The 22-foot-tall reptilian was an extremely quick, vicious, flesh-eating monster. The thirteen dinosaurs charged out of the dungeon to battle the troops with machine guns. Draggono and Taran led the pack of raptors, while the pterodactyls flew high above. As they exited the dungeon, they saw numerous of raptors warring with the troops. Many pterodactyl's were attacking from the air and knocking the armed troops down. As the troops fell or dropped their weapons, the raptors ripped them apart. Draggonosaurus and Tarantulasaurus, Tina, Rebel, and the eleven raptors attacked quickly. They began assisting their associates. Draggonosaurus didn't procrastinate with spitting a large fireball at a group of machine gun shooters. The loud boom was like a bomb, eradicating the troops to smithereens instantly. The firey destruction caused a tragedy, making it easier for the raptors and pterodactyls to prevail. They loved Draggono's superiority and respected him like he was royal.

However, Tarantulasaurus was a different type of animal. The creature hasn't eaten an enormous meal in years. He swung his tail in the direction of a group of armed troops and released a large amount of spider web on approximately 17 soldiers. All of the militants were caught in the sticky web unable to move. Taran ripped the line of web from the end of his tail and yanked it. The 17 troops who were stuck in the sticky web came flying in the air toward the black dinosaur. The

22-foot-tall, four legged dinosaur, jumped in the air and caught all of the humans in his gigantic mouth. He spit a few guns out of his mouth as he crushed the humans, and chewed them up with his huge sharp teeth. The extremely quick reptile, dashed forward speedily, toward another group of armed troops. He was shot dozens of times as he kicked a group of them. The U.S. military members managed to kill many raptors and several pterodactyls.

However, Draggono and Taran exterminated all of the armed troops in less than 5 minutes. Once the semi-battle was concluded, there were only a few pterodactyls and raptors alive. Tina, Rebel were very intelligent King and Queen of their species. They knew survival tactics in tragic battles, to avoid being killed.

"Tina! We're going to need you and the other pterodactyls to fly us out of Las Ventures when we get to the Middle Margin," said Draggono, readily. "Alright Draggono," she replied "Come on you ya'll! Let's get to the Middle Margin," said Draggono, seriously. The huge Draggonosaurus, and Rebel the Raptor led the group toward the Middle Margin. There were only eight other raptors running behind the two elite dinosaurs. Taran and Tina had 6 huge pterodactyls flying behind them as they stomped away toward the Middle Margin. There were a total of 18 manosaurs on the move toward escaping Las Ventures. It was inevitable some of them would escape the invasion, if not all of them. With luck.

With Taran and Draggono guarding, and leading the raptors and pterodactyls, it would take a few more hundred armed troops, with high powered machine guns, to put a end to the destructive Manosaurs.

CHAPTER 6

Escaping Las Ventures

When Megasaur and the others arrived to the Middle Margin, they saw friends they no longer thought existed. Megasaur was shocked to see Timothy the Turtlesaurus and Philip the Frogasaurus, with Stoic and Stacey the Stegosauruses. As they entered into the Middle Margin, they all felt safe. The Middle Margin was a holy dinosaur grounds to them. For some strange reason, powerful spirits of the ancient dinosaurs possessed and protected the place. It was like the armed troops couldn't even see the building. They would pass right over it without acknowledging it. Although the Manosaurs could reside there for awhile, it was risky and the Middle Margin was no place for a Manosaur to live in fear, forever.

Megasaur quickly approached Timothy and Philip and spoke. Timothy was 467 years old, but looked 40, and Philip was 437 old and didn't look at day over 21. "Where have you two been? I haven't seen you two in almost 50 years," said Megasaur. Frogasaurus spoke. "We have been isolated and incognito for decades Megasaur," said Frogasaurus. "But why have you all been hiding? Every Manosaur in Las Ventures thought you two were dead," said Megasaur, in a very deep voice "Because you betrayed me Megasaur! When I went to war with Tarantulasaurus and the pterodactyls, you left me for dead! You and your Tyrannosauruses did not even come and help me in the third war of Las Ventures!," shouted Philip, angrily.

Megasaur was silent for a few seconds. He didn't know how to respond to the genuine allegations. "I did not intervene, because I wanted no parts in the third war, Frogasaurus," said Megasaur, softly. Timothy the Turtlesaurus spoke up. The Turtlesaurus was standing 20 feet tall like always. He almost never crawled and moved slow on four limbs like a typical turtle in this day and age. "How could you not intervene? Philip and I have fought by your side in all of your wars! We fought with you and your father in the first war in Las Ventures! After Tarantulasaurus killed your father and brother, we helped you retaliate and assisted you in the second war. Without us you probably would of been dead and couldn't of exterminate that abomination of dragon species, or put Draggono in Devils Dungeon. But when we went to war with that evil black Tarantulasaurus, you turned your back on us Megasaur! You left all of the Frogasauruses to die! What kind of king would do his allies like that?," said Turtlesaurus, upset.

Megasaur felt ashamed and unroyal. I..... I'm.... I'm sorry you two. At the time, me and my Tyrannosauruses were few in number. My number of army was weak and still rebuilding. Tarantulasaurus had never had more than enough pterodactyls and raptors accompanying him. Over hundreds. We were outnumbered at the time! The third war was a lose-lose battle Turtlesaurus and you know it," said Megasaur. Philip the Frogasaurus spoke and interrupted Megasaur, "You fear Taran! And because of your lack of leadership, all of my Frogasaurus were killed. Turtlesaurus and the Stegosauruses were the only manosaurs that fought by my side and helped me and my kind. Me and my two daughters were the only Frogasauruses that survived. Later Taran commanded the pterodactyls and raptors to kidnap my children a little while later, after the war. I still haven't seen my two little princesses to this day," said Philip, sadly.

He began to reminisce on the tragedy .... Tarantulasaurus, many pterodactyls and many raptors raided the eastside of Las Ventures with intentions to deliberately, kill of all the Frogasauruses. The Frogasauruses were very strong and dominant species of Manosaurs. Their quickness, and ability to pull things with their powerful tongues made them unique. The leaping dinosaurs had a population of forty-four the day of the ambush. Taran was accompanied by King Rebel the Raptor and over 90 raptors. Not to add Tina, Princess of the Pterodactyls, who assisted with over fifty pterodactyls. Although the Frogasauruses were outnumbered they put up a great fight.

Tarantulasaurus knew it would take an army and a navy of Manosaurs to wage war with the elite Frogasauruses. He also knew Turtlesaurus, King Stoic the Stegosaurus, and many Stegosauruses, were going to help the Frogasauruses. It was the biggest and worst war ever in Las Ventures. Megasaur and his Tyrannosauruses did not intervene at all. Much Manosaur blood was shed. Over forty pterodactyls were killed. The Frogasauruses were leaping in the air attacking them; they were snatching them out of the air with their tongue, and crushing them with their strong teeth. Over 60 of the vicious Raptors were killed. The raptors were no imminent threat, or match for a Frogasaurus. They were mainly pawns in the war to keep the battle going while Taran exterminated the majority. Turtlesaurus was the great savior of the war. If it wasn't for Turtlesaurus, the Stegosauruses and the Frogasauruses both, would be extinct. Taran was demolishing his enemies. He was killing Frogasauruses and Stegosauruses left and right, until Turtlesaurus attacked him.

Turtlesaurus was genuinely the unstoppable Manosaur. He was the rightful king and chief of the Manosaurs, but allowed Megasaur to take the throne after his father's death. Turtlesaurus manage to defeat Tarantulasaurus by beating him into submission. Afterward the war quickly came to a end. Philip the Frogasaurus and only two Frogasauruses survived the war. Him and his two daughters; who was still kidnapped later by pterodactyls. Frogasaurus stopped reminiscing about the past quickly as Megasaur spoke.

"Once my Tyrannosauruses reproduced and were strong again, I retaliated for the chaos they caused. That is how I managed to put Tarantulasaurus in iron chains in Devils Dungeon, a few years later," said Megasaur, honestly. "We know Megasaur. But by that time it was too late. The real damage was already done," said Turtlesaurus, truthfully. "Frogasaurus we must get out of Las Ventures and leave while we still have a chance," said Stacey the Stegosaurus. "I agree. Let's get out of here Megasaur," said Brenda, the Brontosaurus.

"You all transform down into your human form, and I will leap all of you right to the top," said Philip the Frogasaurus. Although Frogasaurus was only 22 foot tall he could leap extremely high. However, he could crawl up things very well also. Timothy, Stacey, Stoic, Brenda, Tracey, Chyna, and Little Rex all transformed down into human form. All seven of them were ready for Frogasaurus to leap them out of the underground city, that was under attack. Las Ventures was no longer a safe home and environment for the Manosaurs.

Unfortunately, the real world filled with normal human beings was their only option Tracey looked up at the 25-foot-tall king, still in his dinosaur form. "Megasaur aren't you coming with us," said Tracey, concerned. "No - Tracey! Before I leave Las Ventures, Tarantulasaurus must die! I must avenge my father's death," said Megasaur, in a strange deep voice. "Please Megasaur! Do not stay down here in Las Ventures! We will be lost without you in the real world," said Tracey, sadly. "I can't Tracey. All of you must go on without me. Besides, I have alot of metal from those machine guns in my chest. If I change into human form, it's a matter of time before I would die," said Megasaur. "They have to have humans up there that will help remove the metal Megasaur. Don't stay down here," Brenda said.

Megasaur looked down at the small seven humans that were talking to him. Although he was standing 25 feet tall he could hear the 5 and 6-foot-tall people clearly. "Pa- Pa. Please! If you don't go then I am not going," said little Rex. Without any more discussion, the 7-year-old began transforming and growing into the 8-foot-tall Tyrannosaurus he truly was. Brenda transformed into the 28 foot tall Brontosaurus she was. "Megasaur if you stay, me and little Rex both are staying with you down here," said Brenda. Stoic spoke up. "Make a choice Megasaur! Time is running out! We need to get out of here," said Stoic, seriously. Megasaur contemplated. The huge reptile shook his head made a loud roar, and began decreasing in size. As he transformed down into Marcus, his human form, Brenda and little Rex followed him. All three of the Manosaurs went down to human form. "I'm not going to risk my friends and family. Get us out of here Philip," said Marcus.

The huge Frogasaurus grabbed the 8 small people and concealed all of them in one hand. The 22-foot-tall, green dinosaur, looked up at the roof that lead up to the Society of Las Vegas. He squatted down into a frog like position, and power leaped upward. The gigantic half amphibious reptile balled up his other hand into a fist, and punched the roof as he flew upward toward the roof. The Frogasaurus broke through the thin rocky roof. Small pieces of dirty rock fell downward into the 100 feet deep underground. He landed above the ground in a unknown forest. As the green dinosaur stood up above the trees, he squatted down, released his fellow associates out of his right hand, then he slowly transform down into his human form. The nine Manosaurs looked at one another. It was getting closer to night time and the moon would be appearing in the sky very soon. Marcus, Philip, and Timothy had full moon stones. Brenda, King Stoic, Stacey, Chyna, Tracey and Little Rex did not! They were in grave danger if the moon rose. By them looking at the moon it would make them transform into a violent dinosaur right away. For whatever unknown reason, the moon triggered something inside the Manosaurs, to bring the reptilian out of them. "The moon will be coming up soon Philip! The others are going to need a safe place to hide during the night," said Timothy. "Yes. Then I have to get some help. Those machines have left me with alot of pain. My chest is killing me," said Megasaur. "The rest of you stay here! Timothy, Marcus, and I will go find you all a safe place to hide until the morning time," said Philip.

The other six Manosaur's nodded their heads with understanding. Marcus, Philip

46

and Timothy took off running through the forest full speed, toward the highway. The three Manosaurs were in human form running over 60 miles per hour. The Manosaurs were faster than a cheetah and could reach the max speed of 80 m.p.h., more or less. Their legs were quadruple as strong as a normal human. Their arms were approximately ten or twenty times stronger than a normal human depending on which Manosaur it was. The three reptile humans saw a big semi-truck with a long trailer attached to the back of it. The semi-truck was parked at a rest stop, apparently taking a break.

"If I were a box with wheels; the others can hide in it until the moonlight is gone," said Timothy. "But I don't know how to make it go like they do! Do you?!," asked Philip. "No Philip! But I will learn. I'm 467 years old Philip. Don't forget we were once humans a long time ago," said Timothy, precisely. Timothy was the oldest Manosaur of them all. He was 49 years old the day they found the possessed fossils back in the year 1606 A.D. Timothy hadn't drove a semi-truck ever because they're none that existed seven centuries ago. The three Manosaurs rushed across the highway to the rest stop. They surrounded the semi truck. There was a man inside the truck sleeping. Timothy walked to the driver side door and opened it.

"Hey Man! What are you doing?," shouted the truck driver. Timothy said, "We need this box Sir," the truck driver was reluctant to exit his business truck. "No way man! This is my work truck," shouted the truck driver. Philip opened the passenger side door, leaped inside, and grabbed the truck driver. Philip grabbed him by one of his arms and legs and threw him out of his truck. The man fell to the ground on his buttocks. "Come on Timothy", shouted Philip anxiously. Timothy climbed into the driver seat like he had a C.D.L.'s Once the two Manosaurs were inside, they glanced around looking for Marcus. When Timothy spotted him he said, "Come on Marcus! What are you waiting for?!"

"You two go on without me. I have to get help from the humans before it's too late," said Marcus, in pain. "Are you sure Marcus?" asked Timothy, for reassurance. "Yes Timothy! The moon is coming up! Go save the others," shouted Marcus, without any more discussion, Timothy slammed the door of the semi-truck. They left Marcus right there where he was. Timothy drove the semi-truck as fast as he could without wrecking it.

"The moon is coming up Timothy," said Philip, looking through the windshield window. "I see it. But we're almost there," replied Timothy. It didn't take longer than 60 seconds and they were driving through the forest. As they arrived the other six Manosaur's were beginning to change into their dinosaur form. Being that the moon was hiding behind the dark clouds, the 6 manosaurs weren't effected as much. The moon would be visible for a second, then dark clouds would cover it for a minute, stopping the transformation of the creature. Their dinosaur form was being triggered off and on like a light switch, causing their bones pain. Timothy placed the semi-truck in park; him and Philip exited the truck quickly!

Philip ran to the back of the truck and opened the rear trailer. As the opening rolled upward, Timothy said, "All of you get inside!" No questions were asked. The six manosaurs climbed into the trailer of the semi-truck, when all of them were inside, Philip slammed the retractile rear closed. Timothy looked up and saw the moon visible again.

"I have no idea where we go from here. But life up here is going to be totally different from life in Las Ventures," said Timothy, concerned. Philip looked at him worried. Let's leave here and find a isolated place to remain incognito," said Philip. The two Manosaurs headed to the front of the semi-truck. They entered inside the truck and Timothy ignited it with the turn of the key. Timothy placed the large semi-truck in drive, and the eight manosaurs drove away quickly from the forest. Now they had to do whatever was necessary to survive.

⇨There were alot of Manosaurs rushing into the Middle Margin, to escape Las Ventures. Only problem was the pterodactyls were the only ones with wings to help the others to escape. However, the Manosaurs helped each other. Sergeant Matt and Hank ran behind a huge dinosaur habitat and sat with their backs against the wall. The two military troops refilled their machine guns because they were out of bullets. Tiredly.

"Thank you Sergeant Matt! You saved my life back there. I can't believe we're going to war with dinosaurs," said Hank, seriously. "Well you can start believing it, because you are seeing it for yourself," replied Sergeant Matt. The two member of the U.S. Army shoved the multi-hundred round magazines into their machine guns. They could hear rapid gun shots going on all around them. They were a few yards away from the Middle Margin of Las Ventures. "What the hell has gotten into these people to make them turn into damn dinosaurs?," asked Hank, worried.

Sergeant Matt peeked around the building quickly. He saw a group of dinosaurs headed their way. Sergeant Matt looked back at Hank "Got dammit! I don't know Hank! But we have more company headed this way right damn now," shouted

Sergeant Matt, angrily. Hank glanced around the corner. He saw two-dozen of his armed comrades opening fire on 18 enormous reptiles.

"Not again! I can't wait until this nightmare is over," said Hank, weeping "Shut up Hank and come on! We got to help our men," shouted Sergeant Matt. Sergeant Matt gripped his machine gun tightly and dashed out from the dinosaur habitat. Hank hesitated and did not follow behind the sergeant right away. Sergeant Matt opened fire on an 8-foot raptor that came charging in his direction. The vicious raptor made an extremely loud screeching noise as he raced toward Sergeant Matt. The excellent gun-man aimed the machine gun at the raptors face, pulled the trigger, and many bullets came flying out of the barrel.

Sergeant Matt held the trigger down, and continued shooting at the raptors face. The raptor accepted the bullets and kept charging toward the trooper. As several bullets went into the dinosaurs eyeballs, they penetrated his brain. The huge raptor's body fell on its head, right in front of Sergeant Matt. He looked at the Manosaur closely and saw its body getting smaller. It seemed as if the dinosaur's body was shrinking back down to human form.

Sergeant Matt didn't have much time to pause and conduct a thorough examination due to the war all around him. When he looked up, a long string of sticky spider web struck him in the face. The powerful hit knocked him down on his back, causing him to drop his machine gun. As soon as he fell on his spine, he was snatched right back up. Sergeant Matt went flying through the air as Tarantulasaurus yanked the end of the sticky spider web string. The gigantic black dinosaur caught the troop in his mouth, crushed him with his powerful jaws, and ate him. Hank witnessed the tragedy from behind the building where he was still holding his machine gun hiding.

Although the U.S. troops managed to eradicate a couple raptors and one pterodactyl, all the brave troops were killed within minutes, by the manosaurs. Afraid of death, Hank was the only survivor of that group. He sat behind the dinosaur habitat trembling in fear. Taran, Draggono, Rebel the Raptor, Tina the Pterodactyl, 6 other raptors, and 5 other pterodactyls stomped forward inside the Middle Margin. Before he entered, he spotted a human moving behind a building. The 10-foot-tall reptile blinked his eyes repeatedly to make sure he was seeing precisely.

Rebel the Raptor rushed over to where Hank was sitting. The dinosaur was moving extremely quick and viciously with intentions to devour the human. As the raptor closed in on him, Hank aimed his firearm at the predator. Rebel knocked the gun out of Hanks hand before he could pull the trigger. The creature tried to gobble

Hanks whole body, head first. Half of Hanks body was in the raptors jaws with his feet dangling out. The raptor quickly ripped him apart and ate most of him. In less than 20 seconds, Hank was a full meal to Rebel. The King of the Raptors turned around and quickly headed back into the Middle Margin.

As he entered, he saw eight Manosaurs in their human form, and 6 pterodactyls. Draggono, Taran, and 6 other raptors were in human form, ready to be flown out of Las Ventures by the pterodactyls. Rebel didn't hesitate to transform and shrink down to the 6-foot-tall man he was underneath his gigantic, reptilian appearance. "Tina! You and the pterodactyls fly us up there," said Taran, with, authority. Without deliberation, the 6 pterodactyls grabbed the manosaurs by their shoulders, and flew 6 of them out of Las Ventures. Once they placed the first 6 of them on land, three pterodactyls quickly flew back down, and retrieved the other three manosaurs.

⇨ Marcus met an old man that taught him alot, in a very little time. The old man told Marcus he been shot and drove him to the hospital, quickly. Marcus entered the hospital in severe pain. He was practically stumbling as he walked in. Before he could reach the lovely looking young woman at the desk, he collapsed. The receptionist became worried and panicked right away. She called for nurses and doctors to assist the injured man immediately.

Several medical personnel rushed out into the emergency room with medical equipment to give Marcus assistance. They placed him a hospital stretcher, and pushed him to the back of the hospital, toward the rooming area. The man with a lab coat placed a mask on Marcus's face with high hopes of helping him breath. Marcus quickly fell into a very deep sleep. It was like he was dreaming. He was envisaging event of the first war of Las Ventures.

He saw his father Tyno and his older brother Marvin. The two giant Tyrannosauruses entered into the domain stomping aggressively. "Marcus! Teresa! All of you get up! It's time for us to attack Tarantulasaurus and Draggonosaurus," shouted Tyno, the 25 foot tall T-Rex. Without hesitation, Marcus, Teresa and 10 other Manosaurs in the family stood up.

"Why are we attacking them father?," asked Marcus, curiously. "Don't ask questions Marcus! It's time for war," shouted his father. Teresa and the other 10 Manosaurs transformed into gigantic flesh-eating Tyrannosauruses. While they were growing and evolving, Marcus began changing into the one and only Megasauruses he was. Once the 12 of them were standing over 20 feet tall in their dinosaur form,

King T-Rex told them why they were initiating war. "The brontosauruses has seen the pterodactyls flying 5 baby dragons from pterodactyl cave towards the south. That means that Draggonosaurus has really violated the covenant. He really did fornicate, with the Queen of Pterodactyls, and impregnated her. This will not be tolerated. Draggono and Selena must die! And that new abominating species of fire breathing, flying reptiles, must be annihilated," shouted the great Tyrannosaurus, seriously.

Nobody questioned his royalty. T-Rex looked at his son Marvin. "Marvin did you tell Philip and Timothy to meet us at the Middle Margin?," asked Tyno. "Yes father" replied the Tyrannosaurus, respectfully. "Well then! All of you come on! It's time to put an end to this abomination of Manosaurs," he said. With great ambition the 14 dinosaurs charged out of the domain aggressively. They rushed to the Middle Margin moving at tremendous speed.

When they arrived there, Turtlesaurus and Philip the Frogasaurus was there waiting. The two unique Manosaurs already knew the plan and reasoning for the collaboration, Tyno the Tyrannosaurus greeted them respectfully. "Thank you Timothy! Thank you Philip, for coming to assist me today," said Malcom, showing much gratitude. "You are very welcome T-Rex! We pledge allegiance to you and your Tyrannosauruses, and swore never break our alliance with one another. So you should of known we'd be here," said Philip the Frogasaurus. "Come on you all! Let's teach these rebellious Manosaurs a lesson," said T-Rex, hatefully.

Under no circumstances did anyone debate with Tyno. The 16 dominate dinosaurs moved extremely fast, stomping their way toward the southern end of Las Ventures. The mean reptiles invaded Draggono's lair in the south part of the underground city. Many Manosaurs were present surrounding Draggono. Selena, queen of the pterodactyls was there with her entourage of pterodactyls. Rebel the Raptor was there with a group of raptors, and Tarantulasaurus was there. As Turtlesaurus, Frogasaurus, Megasaurus and the 13 Tyrannosauruses barged in, everyone began transforming into their dinosaur form. Immediately the Royal war began, right inside of Draggonosaurus's lair. Selena shouted to her pterodactyls commanding them to grab her 5 Baby dragons.

"Dactyls! Get my babies out of here! Now!," shouted the Queen Pterodactyl, angrily. Without any contemplating, hesitating, or procrastinating, five large pterodactyls grabbed the baby dragons. Each one of the five flying reptiles snatched a baby dragon, and flew away quickly. Megasaur, his family and associates were pre-occupied fighting their enemies. They didn't even see the 5 pterodactyls fly out of the lair, escaping with the baby dragons. Tyno and Marvin double teamed Tarantulasaurus, while Megasaur and Turtlesaurus double-teamed Draggonosaurus. Teresa, Frogasaurus and the other 10 Tyrannosauruses, attacked Rebel, Selena, and the other raptors, and pterodactyls.

As Frogasaurus snatched Selena by one of her wings, with his tongue, she fell down in front of him. Before Frogasaurus could do anything, Teresa the Tyrannosaurus slaughtered her. The female T-Rex grabbed the oversized pterodactyl with her immense jaws and ripped her apart. Draggonosaurus was very discouraged as he watched his fiancée get killed by the Tyrannosaurus. Draggono was getting conquered by Megasaur and Turtlesaurus. He continued to spit gigantic fireballs at Turtlesaurus. To no avail, the fireballs were ricocheting off Timothy's tough turtle shell everytime.

Turtlesaurus rushed Draggono and dove the sharp pointed edge of his shell into Draggono's chest. Draggono stumbled backward and fell onto his back. While he was on the floor, Megasaur trampled over him. The one horned Manosaur quickly bent down to rip a chunk of flesh out of him. The Draggonosaurus rolled over to avoid the attack, and Megasaur bit him on the neck. The bite was so deadly, it caused Draggono to lose all of his energy. The tall, fire ball spitter started shrinking down to his human form.

Although he wasn't dead, he was in unstable critical condition. He was extremely weak. Too weak to remain in his dinosaur form. When Megasaur glanced to his right, he saw his Tyrannosauruses still fighting several raptors and pterodactyls. Megasaur looked to his left and saw his brother and father tangled in a huge spider web. They were both laying on their backs, and Tarantulasaurus standing over them. He heard Taran whisper.

"Long live the Great King T-Rex." Then the big black dinosaur bit Tyno on his throat, and ripped out his wind pipe. The 8 limbed dinosaur gobbled down the flesh; And quickly did the same to Marvin. Tarantulasaurus killed both of the Tyrannosauruses instantly. Megasaur screamed, "FATHER!"

The Manosaur woke up out of his dream or nightmare screaming loudly. He startled the beautiful female doctor. She dropped her clipboard as she trembled. Angel Nixon looked at Marcus. "Sir calm down! Everything's alright," she assured him. Marcus sat up in the bed, looking around. His body language indicated he lost and confused, and paranoid. "Where the hell am I?," asked Marcus. Angel reached down and picked up her clipboard off of the floor. "You're in the hospital," said Angel, the heart surgeon. Marcus examined himself and his surroundings. "What am I doing in this hospital? It feels like I been asleep for four to five years," replied Marcus, unsure.

It was apparent he had temporary loss of memory, from the coma. He had no idea how long he had been asleep. "Sir what is your name?," asked Angel, clueless. "My name is Marcus Magalino," he said. Angel looked into the dark eyes of the Manosaur and spoke. "Marcus my name is Angel. You come to our hospital a few months ago and collapsed in our emergency room. Sir you had 16 bullets lodged in your chest. Me and my doctors had to conduct an open heart surgery immediately. Right after the surgery you slipped into a coma, and you have been in one for 96 days now Marcus," said Angel, truthfully. Marcus eyes became wide showing the information bothered him.

"What! No! Where's, Teresa and Little Rex?", he blurted out, really questioning himself. "Excuse me? Who are they?," replied Angel confused. "My daughter and my grandson. Has anyone been here to visit me?," asked Marcus, curiously. Angel thought for a second. It had been months since his arrival. She flipped the papers on her clip board looking for any information she could find, concerning his friends and family. "Sorry Marcus! Nobody has come here looking for you. Our 2025 ancestry database has everyone in the world in it, that was born from 1700 on forward. Coincidentally, you are nowhere to be found Marcus. So you're either over 325 years old, or our database is incorrect. And I sincerely doubt our new technology is ever wrong," said Angel seriously. Marcus had to think before responding!

"Your machine has to be wrong. I am 38 years old," replied Marcus, lying. "Well Marcus according to our new medical technology your veins are coming up as 400 years old or more. And your bones and blood are more ancient. The analysis is showing your bones and blood to be millions of years old like you're from the Mesozoic era or something. This is very strange and I would like to do some tests on you," said Angel. Marcus glanced up at her quickly. He was frightened by the information. He knew the intelligent human would be able to realize his identity sooner or later.

Marcus said, "What! This is some type of mistake Angel. Umm … I … I got to get out of here," Marcus quickly got out of the bed. The hospital gown he had on was very thin. "Here Marcus! Take this! Call me if you need my assistance," said Angel, concerned. Angel handed him one of her personal business cards. Marcus hesitated, but grabbed the card without speaking. "Where's my full moon stone?," asked Marcus. Angel pointed toward the shelf behind the hospital bed. "Are you talking about that rock right there," she said.

Marcus turned around and looked in the direction she was pointing in. When he saw the gray stone, he felt relieved. He stepped over and fetched the gray full moon stone. Marcus knew it was his key to survival. He placed on a unfamiliar t-shirt and pants, very quickly. Once he placed his shoes on, he started to head on out of the room. "Hey Marcus!," said Angel, seriously. The Manosaur paused at the door, and looked back at her. "You can trust me. I know what you are. Please call me if you need me out there. I promise I will not betray you," said Angel genuinely. The Manosaur didn't reply or give any indication of how he felt. He nonchalantly departed without showing any emotions towards her.

Angel took a deep breath and slung the clipboard on the hospital bed. She stood in the room thinking. "Be safe you Manosaur. If they find out who you are, they'll kill you right away," whispered Angel, to herself. She knew he was a Manosaur. She knew all about the U.S. Military invading Las Ventures. She knew Marcus was too afraid to trust anyone right then and there. She knew he was not accustom to the normal way of human life. She just wanted to help the handsome looking young man. Although he was antique, he didn't look a day over 35. Her facial expressions showed she was attracted to the half man, half dinosaur man. She just hoped he would believe her words, trust that she wouldn't betray him, and give her a call sooner than later.

Another doctor entered the room where Angel was. The short old British doctor looked in the bed and Marcus was missing. As he rubbed the gray hair on his head, he looked at Angel Nixon. "Doctor Nixon! Where's the young man who was in a coma?," asked Doctor Gladstone. Angel stood up and approached Dr. Gladstone. He was one of the head chemist in charge at the hospital. "Sir I was just about to come and notify you. The patient woke up out of his coma about 3 minutes ago. He was so shocked. He left without getting properly discharged," said Dr. Angel Nixon. "I can't believe this! Do you have any idea where he may be going?," said Dr. Gladstone. "No Doc! I do not! Why? What is it?," said Angel, curiously.

"I have some extraordinary news! I have found something in that man's blood stream that I never seen before, in any human on Earth," said Dr. Gladstone, excitedly. Since Angel knew Marcus was a Manosaur, she found his words to be typical. She expected the doctor to say something she already knew. Coincidentally, he said something she was clueless about. "What is it Doc?"

"His blood has the same molecules as the treatment shot we give our patients at chemotherapy. What's extraordinary is, his blood seems to be more potent, and just may be alot less harmful to the cancer patients," said Dr. Gladstone, smiling. Angel had a look on her face indicating she was shocked by the information. Her mother had died of cancer. News of a potential cure almost brought tears to her eyes immediately. Knowing people would no longer have to suffer like her mother had to, would be a divine blessing. "Oh my God! Are you serious?," said Angel.

"Yes Dr. Nixon! One tube of his blood just might eradicate life threatening cancer out of a human's body. I am going to test it on some children at the chemo cancer treatment center and see. But I have a good feeling his blood just may be the cure for cancer," said Dr. Gladstone. "Alright Doc. I am about to get off work and go home. Please call me and inform me of the results as soon as you get them Dr. Gladstone," said Angel genuinely. "Alright Angel. I will be sure to keep you informed," said Dr. Gladstone. The two doctors exited the hospital room together.

CHAPTER 7

Manosaurs in the Real World

The time was precisely 6:19 post meridiem in Nevada. The eight humble manosaurs were well established now, after 3 months on land. Philip, Timothy, Stoic, Stacey, Brenda, Tracey, Chyna, and little Rex were all living under one roof. The home they had manage to obtain was a 6 bedroom, 3 bathroom that was concealed deep in a forest. The eight manosaurs were surviving the best way they could. They could only roam during the day. At night time they shut all the blinds on the windows to block the moonlight. Since Rex was the only carnivore, he had to go hunt for food. The majority of the time the 8-foot-tall, 7-year-old Tyrannosaurus, would eat animals like; wild hogs, or horses and cows from nearby farm. Rex had lost his mother and was under the impression Megasaur, his grandfather was dead also.

In fact, all of them thought Megasaur was captured or dead. They had waited weeks for him to return. They had even searched the hospitals but had never found him, due to the fact, none of the hospitals had his name in their data base. As time passed, the 8 manosaurs gave up on finding Marcus, and moved on. They had no choice but to find a stable shelter and way to survive.

The time was 6:20 p.m. The other manosaurs looked up as Brenda and Tracey entered the residence, with two enormous bags filled with fruits and vegetables. All the Manosaurs could tell the two ladies had been grocery shopping. Chyna and little Rex stood up and ran toward the adults. Chyna looked into Tracey's eyes. She asked, "Mommy did you bring me anything?," said her 6 year old daughter.

Tracey smiled and said, "Yes Chyna. I brought your favorite fruits," "Please tell me you brought a lot this time Mommy," said Chyna. "Chyna we do not have money like that honey! 50 apples and 50 oranges are going to have to be enough for today," said Tracey, seriously. Philip, Timothy, Stoic and Stacey were sitting at the table in the dining room. "Here you are little Rex", said Brenda. The 7-year-old boy smiled as he accepted the bag filled with pounds of bloody raw uncooked meat.

"Thank you, Brenda," he said. The two children grabbed the large bags of food and didn't struggle to carry them outside. The two kids took the bags of food out toward the back yard, where they would transform into their dinosaur form and eat. Since they were residing far off in the woods, surrounded by trees, the manosaurs didn't have to worry about any neighbors seeing them in their ultimate form. Their nearest neighbor was a farmer living in the woods over 200 yards away.

The six adults remained in the mansion discussing their means of survival and maintaining their establishment. "We cannot continue to live in fear like this! We barely have any money! We can barely feed ourselves, and the two kids!" said Brenda, seriously. "Brenda I have given you one of my full moon stones! You don't even have to feed yourself. The blue moon stone will absorb minerals from the moon and keep you full," said Philip, immediately. "I understand that Philip! But these children eat over 150 pounds of food a piece every day. And what about Stoic, Stacey, and Tracey. They have no full moon stones," said Brenda.

Stoic spoke up from the table. Stacey and Stoic were seated directly across from Philip and Timothy. "Stegosauruses are different Brenda! We can live comfortable off the grass and trees every day," said Stoic. Tracey spoke right afterward. Her and Brenda was still standing up near one another. "Listen Stoic! You and Stacey have no children! I have to take care of Chyna. And now that Megasaur is dead or lost, Brenda has taken care of little Rex being his responsible guardian. I mean ... we love our children and only want the best for them. We don't want our children to live in poverty, fear and be afraid of humans," said Tracey, frustrated. "You have no choice Tracey!,' shouted Stoic.

"We do have a choice! We need to quit hiding in these damn woods like cowards! And get out there and accomplish success," shouted Tracey, upset. All of the adult Manosaurs were silent. Tracey had made a bold statement that all of them knew to be true. "Tracey has a good point," said Stacey, Stoic's wife. Stoic stood up quickly and began shouting. "She does not! This is not our land! This is not our home! What part of that you don't understand! If you go out there trying to be brave, and fit in with those humans, it's only a matter of time before they follow you right back here, track you down and kill us all Tracey," said Stoic, intelligently.

Timothy spoke up. "He's absolutely right Tracey. It's not about being brave. It's about being intelligent and not ignorant. I say we lay low until Las Ventures is safe to return and live again," said Timothy. The two women were shaking their heads in disagreement. "I'll never go back! Over a hundred Manosaurs were killed right before my eyes. I don't ever want to see Las Ventures again," said Tracey. Brenda spoke up in agreement. "Neither do I. Besides, Tarantulasaurus and Draggonosaurus will only kill us if we return. And if they are up here in the real world, who's to say they won't return to Las Ventures again one day," said Brenda.

They all were silent again for a moment. Philip broke the silence. "Going back to Las Ventures is not a option. We face death and extinction by humans and Tarantulasaurus, if we go back. All of you are right in your own way. Sooner or later, we have to be brave, go out and accomplish better things. However, we must be extremely careful not to bring trouble back to our secret residence," said Philip, with leadership.

⇨ Chyna the 6-year-old Triceratops, was in the backyard with Little Rex, the Tyrannosaurus. The two children had transformed and enlarged into their secondary form. Chyna was busy eating the apples and oranges her mother Tracey had bought her. Little Rex had gobbled down most of the raw bloody meat Brenda had produced for him from the grocery store. As Rex was out of food he looked over at Chyna. Chyna noticed the 8 foot Tyrannosaurus was finished with his dinner extremely quick. She glanced up as the 7-year-old T-Rex came her way. "Rex you're done already!," said Chyna astonished. "Yeah Chyna. They never buy us enough food! I'm still hungry," said little Rex, sadly.

Chyna looked down at her fruits on the ground. She still had approximately twenty apples and thirty oranges lying on the ground in front of her. "Would you like some of my food Rex?" She said, very nicely and kindly. Little Rex looked down at the unpleasing herbivore delicacy. "No thank you Chyna! I don't like that kind of food. It hurts my tummy," replied little Rex, frowning. Chyna ate a few more oranges and apples off of the ground and looked up at the 8-foot-tall Tyrannosaurus. "Are you sure Rex? These one's taste really good," she added sweetly. Rex shook his head, and walked away. As little Rex wandered off into the woods, Chyna continued eating the rest of her fruits. After a couple minutes, the baby triceratops began glancing around for her best friend. She galloped toward the woods in the direction Little Rex ran off in.

As she entered the woods, she said, "Hey Rex! Where are you?" Chyna continued on searching and began going further and further into the deep woods. She knew she was way out of the territory the adult Manosaurs had warned them to remain in. Although she was out of Manosaur boundaries, her worries about little Rex caused her to continue, moving further into the woods. "Rex! Where are you?," She screamed, loudly. The 6-year-old female Manosaur changed her appearance. She quickly began minimizing down into her little girl form.

The 6-year-old girl saw a huge farm as she reached another part of the woods. She saw a huge red barn, a silo with a cone top, and sheep in the barnyard. There were several horses and cow's walking around the farmland also. Chyna heard Rex's voice in her head. "They never buy us enough food! I'm still hungry," was the words of little Rex. Although Chyna couldn't see Rex, he was on the other side of the red barn. Chyna began walking towards the barnyard. Rather she knew it or not, her and Rex trespassed onto the farmer's private property.

Little Rex was in his human form, stalking a cow. The large black and white mammal watched the 7-year-old little boy carefully out the corner of her eye. Rex glanced around, observed his surroundings, then began transforming into his dinosaur form. The cow began mooing as she saw the 8 foot vicious and hungry reptile. As the cow began mooing and moving away, Rex attacked her. The savage young Tyrannosaurus tackled her from behind and clawed her, Rex bit the cow on the neck with his strong sharp teeth, and ripped a nice chunk of flesh out of the cow. Without remorse, Rex swallowed the chunk of meat and bit her again.

The young T-Rex was on top of the cow eating her voraciously. The cow was lying on her side bleeding with chunks missing from her body. Rex was enjoying his meal. He didn't notice the huge bull that was charging towards him. The bull was seconds away from ramming his two sharply pointed horns, into Rex's spine. Before the bull could complete his intended attack, he was hit in the side by a triceratops. The male bovine animal, fell to his side, injured critically. The 3 sharp horns that were rammed into the bull by the triceratops left 3 big holes in the bull's rib cage.

Rex raised up off of the cow he had devoured with blood dripping from his jaws. Rex looked at Chyna, realizing she had saved him from the bull's ambush. "Rex what are you doing? We have to get out of here before we get into trouble," said Chyna, seriously. "Alright Chyna. Just let me finish eating the rest of my food," said

Rex. Chyna glancing around like she was a look out for them. While Rex finished ripping the flesh of the cow with his huge teeth, the young triceratops observed their surroundings. The owner of the farm came out of his home with a double-barrel shotgun, he scared the triceratops. Chyna screamed as her eyes were filling with fear, and impending danger.

"Rex let's go! He's got a gun," shouted Chyna terrified. The young dino was afraid of guns. She had saw enough of her kind die by guns that dismember manosaurs. Rex stood up immediately with blood covering his huge sharp teeth and jaws.

The farmer said "What the hell is that thing?," the farmer cocked his double barrel shotgun, as he ran off of the porch. As the two dinos began charging away, the farmer pulled the trigger discharging the shotgun at Little Rex in particular. The farmer shot Rex in the side of his right leg with the shot gun, injuring him instantly. He almost fell down as he was shot, and tried to continue fleeing. "Rex!," shouted Chyna, horrified. Her eyes became wide open and filled with devastation. The farmer moved toward and cocked the shot gun again. As he aimed the shot gun at the female triceratops, a huge green dinosaur leaped down out of the air.

The 22-foot-tall creature shook the ground, as he landed in front of the farmer. The gigantic Frogasaurus discharged his long and powerful tongue at the farmer. The huge sticky tongue wrapped around the farmer's whole body like a long snake. Frogasaurus squeezed the farmer, and snatched the human back towards him. His enormous long tongue came flying back in his mouth with the farmer wrapped at the end of it. The Frogasaurus chewed up the human, spit the shot gun out on the barnyard, and looked at the two dino's. Chyna was smiling as Philip the Frogasaurus saved their lives. When she saw Frogasaurus was angry, and not smiling, she looked disappointed.

The huge dinosaur dropped down on all fours to avoid standing taller than the trees around them. He moved forward to the other two dino's. Chyna could tell he was not happy. "What are you two doing here Chyna! Didn't we tell you both, not to leave our territory!," shouted the huge green dinosaur, angrily. Chyna put her head down and spoke. "I know Frogasaurus. But I was only looking for Rex," she said, softly. Rex struggled to walk. He was bleeding badly. "Rex! You intentionally disobeyed what we told you not to do," said Frogasaurus, upset, "I know Frogasaurus. I am sorry," said Rex, sadly. "You should be Rex! You could of been killed! And even worst, you could of got Chyna killed also," said Frogasaurus, upset.

"I'm sorry. I was hungry and just trying to get some more food to eat. I didn't mean for none of this to happen," said little Rex, very, sadly. "Get home now Rex!," shouted Frogasaurus. The green dinosaur stood patiently as the two dinos hurried back home. Rex was injured but managed to stomp quickly behind the galloping triceratops. As Frogasaurus looked up, he saw the moon coming out into the dark sky.

The huge amphibious reptilian power leaped very high in the air. He landed two hundred yards away right near their home. He shook the ground as he landed in the backyard of their 6-bedroom home. He began minimizing back down to his human form. Once he was fully turned into Philip, he walked into the home.

⇨ The sky was dark like an abyss, but the moonlight night was visible. The time was 9:14 at night, and Las Vegas was very populated. Marcus was wandering through the city on feet like a stray dog. He continued turning around, and watching his surroundings, like a paranoid person would. Marcus was unfamiliar with the atmosphere and environment. He had nowhere to go, no money in his possession and no clue where his family was. Or Little Rex at least.

The others were merely very close friends and associates. Marcus saw a semi-truck with a trail that looked like the one Timothy and Philip had stolen three months ago. As the truck headed his way, Marcus ran into the middle of the road. He stuck both of his hands out indicating for the truck driver to stop. The man driving the huge semi-truck came to a halt, the driver slammed on the brakes to avoid hitting Marcus. As the truck driver rolled down his window he spoke! "What's your problem man? Get out of the damn road!," shouted the truck driver. Marcus walked to the driver side of the truck. "I'm looking for my family. Are they in the back of this truck?," asked Marcus, seriously. "Your family! Now why in the hell would they be in the back of my semi-truck," shouted the truck driver. "May I take a look?," asked Marcus.

"No Man! I'm leaving," replied the man. The man began to drive away. Before the semi-truck caught great speed, Marcus ran and jumped on the back of the truck. While the truck was moving, the strong Manosaur grabbed the handle of the trailer. Unknowing how to open the retractor, Marcus ripped the whole back off the trailer. When he saw a bunch of boxes, he was disappointed and jumped off the semi-trailer.

The truck driver pressed the brakes, slowed down, and stopped the truck. He opened the driver side door and exited the vehicle. He saw the back piece of his trailer in the middle of the road, as Marcus was running away. "How in the hell did he yank the whole door off like that?," said the truck driver.

Marcus ran for his life, not knowing if the man had a gun or what he would do to him. He had no idea why humans operated the way they did or reacted to situations. Marcus saw a 32-year old man enter into a liquor bar. As the man walked in, Marcus yelled. "Philip! Philip is that you?," shouted Marcus. The man didn't respond, and closed the door behind him. Marcus began running toward the bar. As he approached the bar, two ladies were entering. He walked in right behind them. One of the petite, blonde haired women, looked at Marcus, up and down, from head to toe. "Hello there handsome," said the pretty Barbie looking woman.

Marcus barely smiled, nodded at her, and continued looking for Philip. Marcus didn't look old, due to the fact all Manosaurs barely ever aged physically. Although they appeared young, their organs and mentality could be hundreds of years old. When Marcus spotted the man he thought was Philip, he ran up to him. Marcus grabbed the man by the shoulder. "Philip", said Marcus.

The tall boldman pushed Marcus off of him. "Get your hands off of me you weirdo!," said the man. As he pushed Marcus, the Manosaur stumbled backwards into a muscular motorcycle rider. He made the huge 6 foot 6-inch-tall, 265 pound red neck, spill his glass of expensive liquor. The red neck became angry immediately.

He stood up, grabbed Marcus, and slammed the Manosaur on top of a wooden table. The table broke in half as Marcus crashed on top of it. Although he was hurt, he managed to get back up again. Four other red necks who was a part of the motorcycle gang, surrounded Marcus. Marcus looked around at the 5 white men, dressed in black jackets, with black bandanas around their heads. "Listen man! I didn't come here looking for trouble," said Marcus, worried. "Well guess what chump! You sure as hell found trouble," shouted one of the drunken men.

The pretty young lady behind the counter picked up her phone, called the police, and told them it was a brawl going on at the bar. The biker gang members had no idea the bartender had called the cops to come.

One of the men swung a closed fist at Marcus. The Manosaur ducked the punch, grabbed the man and slung him away to the other side of the bar. Other bystanders were amazed by the herculean ability. "Oh so you think you're a tough guy huh! Well I guess B.B.W.B. is going to have to teach you a lesson," shouted the man, as he ripped off his shirt. The man began cracking his knuckles indicating he was going to punch, and pound Marcus. The huge red neck cracked his neck as he moved it from side to side.

"Come on and get you a piece of the Big Bad White Boy!" shouted the man, as he walked towards Marcus. His fist was balled up and out in front of him. He swung at Marcus with his left hand, and Marcus caught the fist with his left hand. The Big Bad White Boy swung with his right and punched Marcus in the face. The hard hit affected Marcus to the point, he leaned sideways. Marcus did not fall. Instead, the repercussion was an uppercut right to B.B.W.B.'s face. Marcus hit the huge muscular gang member as hard as he could with the right hand uppercut. B.B.W.B. went flying through the air backwards landing on his back. Many people in the bar could see that Marcus was extra-ordinary strong. The other three bikers did not want to fight Marcus after they witnessed his capabilities.

As Marcus ran out of the bar, the police were exiting their cars. 6 policemen exited out of 4 police cars. One of the squad cars had two officers get out of it. "Hey you! Freeze!," shouted the police officer. Marcus was afraid when a couple of the officers pulled out guns. Although he was under the impression they were aiming guns at him, the officers had exotic tazors in hand. Marcus paused for a moment. After contemplation, he decided to flee for his life. The Manosaur moved extremely fast as he dashed in the direction he saw was a passage way. Two of the officers pulled the triggers of their electrocution guns at Marcus! As the metallic and electricity went into Marcus body, he fell to the ground.

The other officers ran into the bar to arrest the other trouble makers. It didn't take long for the policemen to place Marcus in handcuffs, and put him in the backseat of the police car. As the officers slammed the back door, Marcus came to realization he had been captured. Doing everything to avoid showing his true identity, he tried to break the handcuffs. Unfortunately, he was too weak to do so.

Marcus began panicking uncontrollably knowing he had to escape the approaching, life threating danger, he was left with no choice; Marcus began roaring extremely loud and transforming into his dinosaur form. His roar could be heard for miles away in a silent city. All eyes were on the police vehicle as they realized it was where the dangerous sound was coming from. Before they could talk and go over to the squad car, a huge dinosaur started ripping through the roof of the car! The police officers pulled out their guns as the 25-foot-tall Megasaurus, grew larger, and totally destroyed the car.

Megasaur gave a loud roar as he stepped on a police car crushing it in half with one gigantic stomp. A horrifying look was in the officers eyes. It was obvious they wanted to run for their lives instead of being brave. However, being brave would cost them their lives.

The police officers began firing their pistols at Megasaur and shooting him with small bullets. Megasaur was used to high powered artillery with much more force and bullets. The minutiae weapons only made Megasaur angrier. The gigantic Manosaur gave off a loud roar, as he picked up the destroyed police car, and slung it in their direction. The police began to run and flee, along with all the other civilians who were in the vicinity. People were yelling and screaming, and running for safety. Filled with hate and rage Megasaur started striking buildings with great force. The unknown dinosaur began shattering things and causing major destruction to everything he came in contact with.

The 25-foot-tall creature stomped on cars like they were Lego's to him. It was obvious the Megasaurus was furious. But it was more than the cops, and the fight in the bar, that had him on a violent collusion with anything in his path. It was the death of Teresa. The thought of never seeing Little Rex again. The thought of how the humans of the military had invaded Las Ventures and tried to eradicate his species. Megasaur slaughtered many cars, buildings, people, places and things, until he became exhausted. Once he was tired he came back down to his human form, and began running far away.

The manosaur ran almost 56 miles per hour for a half minute. When he reached a place where he felt safe, he fell down to the ground, and sat. Marcus was breathing extremely hard. He had a couple bullet wounds on his arm when he examined himself. However, they were nothing fatal, and his dinosaur form had accepted the majority of the damage. The bullets hadn't penetrated down into his human body like the military weapons did, down in Las Ventures.

"I got to find Angel. I need somebody's help," said Marcus to himself.

CHAPTER 8

Marcus and Angel Meet Again

Rebel, Taran and Draggono sat at a table discussing masterplans of conquering their surroundings. The three Manosaurs were in their human form and talking very civilized. The 3 reptile-men were very intelligent. They had managed to achieve a mansion for themselves, and their comrades to reside in. There were a total of 15 manosaurs and 6 of them females. Three of the women were raptors, and three of them were pterodactyls.

Tina, Princess of the Pterodactyls, and the other 5 women were asleep in their rooms. Rebel, Taran, and Draggono were the only three awake, because it was pass eleven o'clock at night. The 6 other men in the mansion were either lying in bed asleep beside their women or very comatose. "I haven't seen or heard anything from the 5 renegade Tyrannosauruses. I know they are long gone to take some more riches. They were running low on money," said Taran seriously.

Rebel took a sip of his alcoholic drink in his glass, before he spoke. "Yeah, me and the raptors were going out tonight to take some valuables, but we changed our minds," replied Rebel. "Well tomorrow! We all must get off our asses and go out to take the things we need from these humans."

"We have nothing at all," said Taran, discouraged. "What we need to do is take the money and buy alot of farm animals," said Rebel, being wise. "That's not a bad idea. Breeding horses, pigs, chickens, goats, and cattle would be a wise plan. Therefore, we'd always have food. What you think about that Draggono?," asked

Taran. Draggono wasn't even listening to them, or paying them any attention. He was thinking about his own goal and priorities.

"Huh! What did you say?," he asked completely lost. "What! Are you not listening Draggono?," said Taran. "Honestly I was thinking about something else," replied Draggono. Taran picked up his cup of liquor and took a drink. He swallowed the alcohol quickly and exhaled loudly. "So what the hell are you over there plotting and planning Draggono?," said Taran. "I want a full moon stone Taran! I can't continue to run in the house every night like some adolescent with a curfew! We must find Megasaur, Frogasaurus, and Turtlesaurus! We need full moon stones!," said Draggono, aggressively.

"Don't challenge destiny Draggono! We will find those weaklings and take those full moon stones! Just be patient my friend. It's only a matter of time. But I promise you! We will both have full moon stones in due time," said Taran, seriously. Discouraged and anxious Draggono finally swallowed a big gulp of liquor from his glass. As he chugged a nice amount of alcohol; Rebel spoke. "Easy there Draggono! That liquor is potent. I will burn your chest," said Rebel. "My mother was Albinosaurus Rebel! I spit fire! This liquor is like ice water to me. It can't burn my chest," said Draggono.

"You know something, I've always wondered. How come can you spit fireballs but Megasaur cannot?," said Taran, curiously. "I don't know Taran. I guess I took more out of our mother's blood line. And Megasaur took after his father Tyrannosaurus, D.N.A.," replied Draggono. "Well I guess that makes sense," replied Taran. The trio was interrupted by a beautiful young female. Rebel when are you coming to bed and lay with me?," asked the female Manosaur. The three leaders of the group glanced over at the female raptor, in her human form.

"Give me a minute Rebecca. I will be there shortly," replied Rebel. "Alright Rebel! Last time I checked. I was your wife, not Taran or Draggono," said Rebecca, upset. Draggono shouted, "Don't you start Rebecca!" She looked at Draggono and replied, "You don't start! You should be in the bed with your woman, Tonya! And Taran, should be lying next to Tina. Instead! You three are up here drinking and plotting on foolishness," she said, aggressively. As she walked away, Taran shouted. "Plotting on foolishness is what got you women this lovely mansion." The three Manosaurs continued sitting at the huge round table.

"Well fellows. I better get going before I get put on a restriction, if you know what I mean!," said Rebel. Taran smiled at the comment. I agree. I think I'm going to head upstairs with Tina also," said Taran. "Tomorrow we must go take," said Taran, again. The two Manosaurs were wobbly as they walked toward their destination. Draggono didn't leave the table. He remained there meditating. He whispered to himself. "Your right Taran. Take a full moon stone. Everything else is futile."

* March 17th, 2025

Dr. Gladstone arrived at the cancer treatment center around 7:00 ante meridiem. He parked his all white Bentley Continental in the parking lot of the place, reached inside the glove compartment and grabbed his last two tubes of Marcus blood. He had already used the first tube of blood to conduct test which led him to believe Marcus's blood was a potential cure for cancer.

Dr. Gladstone had contacted the Cancer Treatment Center to see if anyone would agree and consent to injecting to potential cure in their human body. Although he could have easily tested the blood on an animal, he wanted to insert it into a living human body, and see the results. He opens the door of his luxury car, exited, and locked the doors. He quickly placed his all white lab coat over his body and headed toward the entrance. As he walked inside, he was greeted respectfully by the head cancer therapeutic.

"Hello there Dr. Gladstone!," said the doctor, as he entered. "Hey there Dr. Tulip," replied Dr. Gladstone, smiling. "Listen Doc. I have a lady and her husband who has come forward, and volunteered to allow the potential cure to be tested on their twins," said Dr. Tulip. "What!" replied Dr. Gladstone, excitedly. "Yeah! They have already signed the proper paper work and waivers. The two children are up stairs and ready to begin now," he said. "My God," said Dr. Gladstone. "Yeah Doc. And it's bad too! The cancer is really killing these two poor little children," replied Dr. Tulip, sadly.

"Well Dr. Tulip, I am ready to start. I don't want to waste another second talking. If these two tubes of blood is a potential cure, I am ready to find out," replied Dr. Gladstone seriously. Dr. Tulip began smiling. He placed both of his hands together, and nodded at him. "Come on then Dr. Gladstone. Let's go to where the twins are." The two doctors began walking side by side down the main hallway of the Cancer Treatment building.

They took an elevator upstairs to the laboratory where the two sick children were being held at. The men dressed in white lab coats opened the door of the lab, and entered inside. Immediately, Dr. Gladstone noticed the little boy and girl lying in the bed resting. They were already hooked up to the diagnostic machines that were examining their small bodies regularly. It was obvious they were fighting and battling cancer from their appearance. Their hairless heads and fragile looking bodies, verified the disease was in them.

⇨ Since Angel woke up late, the kids wouldn't have to go to school today. It was 9:00 A.M. when Angel got out of her bed. The beautiful, long haired woman with blue eyes, placed her robe around her waist, and headed out of the room. As she went down stairs, she saw Abagail brushing her Barbie dolls hair. Her son Anthony was playing a video game.

"Anthony it's my turn to play! I want to play the game too," said Abagail, sadly. Anthony had just lost and refused to give up the controller. "Alright Abbie! Just let me try this stage one more time," said Anthony. Abagail inhaled and blew her breath very loudly. She folded her arms and frowned, indicating she was tired of her brother pushing her off. "I'm telling Mommy!," she shouted. "So Abbie! It's my game, not yours," he replied. As Abagail stood up and glanced around, she was startled by her mother's presence. Abagail twitched, and moved spasmodically, not knowing her mother was standing right behind them.

"Mom! Anthony won't let me play the video game," said Abagail, sad and sympathetically. Her mom looked at her unconcerned about the video game. "Why didn't one of you wake me up so I could take you two to school?," asked Angel, disappointed. Abagail shrugged her shoulders and said, "I don't know! I thought you were the grown up and make all the decisions around here! Remember," said Abagail, sarcastically. "Hey little girl! Don't get sassy with me," replied Angel, meanly.

"I'm not getting sassy Mommy. But that's your responsibility to get up and take us to school," said Abagail, smartly. Angel walked away toward the kitchen. "Whatever Abbie! I guess you're right," shouted Angel, loudly, as she walked into the kitchen. Abagail followed her towards the kitchen and sat down at the table. Angel grabbed a glass of orange juice and began drinking. She looked at Abagail out of her peripheral vision. Angel quickly walked out of the kitchen intentionally to get a reaction out of her daughter. She knew Abagail was hungry for breakfast and waiting for her to cook.

"Mom! Where are you going?," shouted Abagail. Angel glanced back and replied, "I'm going back to my room and going back to sleep," said Angel, with a smirk on her face. "But Moommmm! We're hungry! We haven't even ate breakfast," said Abagail. "Well Abagail; If you would of woke me up at 7:00, I would of cooked a nice breakfast for you all, like I do every morning. Since you guys manipulated your way out of school today. I'll let you two start making the decisions around now," she said, sarcastically. Angel continued walking away. Abagail emerged from the glass dining room table and followed her mother. "But Mom! I don't know how to cook!," shouted Abagail, sadly.

"The way you talk to me. I thought you was a grown up round-here. So if you want me to keep cooking for you every day. You need to stop talking back to me and being sassy Abagail," said Angel, seriously. Abagail lowered her head and said, "I'm sorry Mommy. I won't do it again," said Abagail, sadly. "Alright Abbie. Don't let it happen again," replied her mother.

Angel went upstairs and got dressed. She came back down and began cooking breakfast for her two children. Abagail sat at the table watching her mother cook from a distance. It wasn't long before Angel was finished preparing the morning meal. She brought two nice plates to the table and sat them down. "Anthony! Put that video game on pause, and come eat your breakfast," shouted Angel. The 13-year-old boy paused the game right then, and headed toward the dining area. He sat down in front of the nice plate of food.

"Thanks Mom," said Anthony, respectfully. "Thank you Mommy," added Abagail, right after. The plate was filled up with several breakfast desires. Angel had cooked them scrambled eggs, cheesy grits, pancakes with chocolate chips in the middle, bacon, sausage, and an omelet on the side. She brought butter and syrup to the glass table for them. The family said the grace and prayed together before eating, like always. Once they all said Amen, in unison, they began eating, like always. The kids were hungry and began gobbling the food down like they haven't ate in days. "Mommy you're the best chef in the world," said Abagail, with a mouth full of food.

"I wouldn't say all of that. I think you're trying to butter me up, so I'll keep cooking for you all," said Angel, smiling. Abagail swallowed her food before she spoke again. "No Mom! I'm not. You really are the best cook I've ever had," said Abagail. "Well that's probably because I'm the only person who cooks for you, besides the McDonalds you always want," she replied. Their conversation was interrupted by the doorbell. Angel stood up from the table, and started walking towards the front door. She peeked through the window, and saw Marcus standing outside. She was surprised he appeared at her residence. "Marcus!", she whispered. She ran back into the dining area where the kids were. The two children had a look of curiosity on their faces.

"Who was at the door Mom?," asked Anthony, the 12 year old. "Doesn't matter! I need you two to go to your rooms now!," said Angel, seriously. Abagail said, "But why do we have to go to our rooms Mommy?," asked Abagail. "Because I said so Abbie! Didn't we just have this discussion about talking back to me and being sassy," said Angel, seriously. "Okay Mom," replied Abagail. As the kids got up from the table, the door bell rung again. Angel watched as her nosey young children proceeded upstairs to their room. "And stay in there until I say you can come out! Or it's going to be trouble," said Angel. Although Angel had never physically disciplined her children, they didn't know what, 'it's going to be trouble' meant.

Once the children were out of sight, and in their bedroom, Angel ran back to the front door. She didn't want any new random man around her children. Although she could tell Marcus was a good person with nice characteristics, she would have to get to know him personally before introducing her kids to him.

Angel opened the front door and looked into the eyes of Manosaur. "Marcus what are you doing here?", she asked. "You told me to contact you if I need your help. And I need your help Angel," he replied. "Why didn't you call me before coming?," she asked. "Because I have no phone or no money. And I am scared to trust these humans," said Marcus, worried. Angel glanced behind her to make sure her children were nowhere in sight. "Come in Marcus!," she whispered.

Angel closed the door as Marcus entered. Marcus looked around the home observing everything. "This is quite a small house," said Marcus. Coincidentally Angel had a nice size home. 4 bedroom, 3 bathroom, 800,000 $ dollar, two story, luxurious home. You have to be joking," she replied, surprised by the comment. "Well I'm used to homes ten times bigger than this," replied Marcus, honestly.

He was solely referring to the dinosaur habitats, and domes in Las Ventures. "Of course you are! I've saw those remarkable kingdoms you Manosaurs lived in down in Las Ventures," said Angel. Marcus shouted! "You've been to Las Ventures!," Angel replied, "Oh God No! I seen them on the internet."

Marcus had no idea what the internet was. He had no idea what a computer was. He had no idea what none of the new creations were. He had been underground since the day he was born in 1608 A.D. "What is the internet?," asked Marcus genuinely. She looked at Marcus like he was ignorant or just plain crazy. "You got to be kidding me Marcus. Be honest how old are you Manosaurs?," she asked, curiously. Marcus was reluctant to be truthful. He hesitated to speak, not really wanting to trust her.

"Listen Marcus, you have to start trusting somebody, and right now, I am all you have!," said Angel, seriously. "I guess your right Angel. Truthfully, I am 417 years old," he said. "Whoooah." She said. "You know what Marcus! I knew it from the blood test! But what I don't understand is why do you look my age," she replied. "How old are you," he asked. "Marcus! Your not supposed to ask a woman her age," she replied. "And why is that? You just asked me my age."

"Because Marcus! You just don't. But since you told me your age, I am 36," said Angel. "Angel, Manosaurs don't age physically on the outside. We are on the inside. Although I look like I am in my thirties, I'm over twenty times older than you," he replied. "Well the internet is the way we humans find out anything we need to know. The internet knows everything in the world," said Angel, smiling. "Really! Please take me to meet the internet. Maybe he can help me find my family and friends," said Marcus, relieved. Angel looked at Marcus in a foolish way.

"Hold up! Wait; wait, wait Marcus. The internet is not a real person," she said. "What! So why did you just lie to me?," he said, upset. "No Marcus! I didn't lie to you. The internet is a computer," she said. "So what is a computer?," he said curiously. Angel glanced up stairs and saw her kids peeking downstairs. They were trying to confirm if their mother was seeing another man, since the death of their father last year. "Go to your rooms!" Shouted Angel, very loud.

The kids scattered like kittens in fear. Marcus looked upstairs and saw the children vanish. "You have children," said Marcus, curiously "Yes two of them. What about you?," asked Angel. "Yes I had one," he replied. "What do you mean had one?," she asked, "Teresa was killed by the humans with guns when they came in Las Ventures to kill all of my kind," replied Marcus, sadly. "I am sorry to hear that Marcus. You're not the only one who survived!," she said. "I know Angel! There are other Manosaurs who escaped out of Las Ventures. Some of them are my friends and family. I need you to help me find them," said Marcus.

Angel's nose began to fidget and move nervously. She began sneezing uncontrollably. Marcus just looked without saying God bless you. Unfortunately, he had no idea of the motto. "Marcus you really are naive, to the way the world works today. When people sneeze, you are supposed to say God bless you," she said.

Marcus nodded. "Okay. I'll remember that next time," he replied. "Now listen! I don't know how you all used to do it down there in Las Ventures, but we have to take a bath with soap and water up here. So you need to clean yourself and I will give you some of my husband's old clothes to put on," she said.

"You're married!," said Marcus, shocked. "Yes and no. My husband is dead. He died in a car crash last year. Him and my youngest son," "Oh" said Marcus. "Come on, follow me. You don't have nothing to worry about," said Angel. She stood up and lead Marcus upstairs to her bedroom so he could take a shower.

They entered her bedroom, and walked in her master bathroom. She walked over to the shower, turned the warm water on, and prepared everything for the unintelligent individual. Well Marcus was very smart. Technology was just too advanced for him to catch up with it in one day. "So tell me exactly, how this thing works," he said. Well you just get inside of it, and let the water spray all over your whole body. Wait right here! Let me go get you a new washcloth to bathe with," said Angel.

She quickly exited the bathroom and fetched a towel, and washcloth for Marcus. She closed the closet back, and headed back to the bathroom. When she entered back into the bathroom, Marcus was naked and underneath the water that was spraying out of the shower head. She looked at Marcus, as he looked at her. "My God, Marcus! Why didn't you wait?," she said, rhetorically. She tried to cover her eyes with her left hand, as she handed him the washcloth. After a glimpse of his attractive body, she was mesmerized by his well-built body.

Use that soap right there, and rub it all over your body, use the wash cloth to wipe your whole body down. And when you get out of the water, use this towel right here to get all the rest of the water off of you," she said. "Okay Angel. Thank you," said Marcus. Angel looked back at Marcus naked body again. "My God he has a nice body," she said to herself.

Angel exited the bathroom, and laid in her bed. She turned the television on, which was already programmed to the news channel. She immediately saw breaking news. Angel saw an enormous dinosaur on the news destroying buildings, cars, and people violently. "Oh my God! What is this?," she said. Angel turned up the volume up so she could hear the words of the news reporter.

Ladies and Gentlemen's please be careful. Some of these dangerous creatures have managed to escape from underneath the ground and have come up on land. They can easily be mistaken for a normal human being. However, they are not normal. These creatures we call manosaurs, are very unpredictable. Citizens of Nevada, please be extremely cautious! This is the fifth dinosaur rampage of a Manosaur. No arrests or killing of the creatures has yet to be made," said the female news reporter. "Thank you for the information Margret," said a male news reporter. "Also coming up. We have a speech from the general of the U.S. Armed Forces, concerning Manosaur's in America," said the male reporter.

Angel changed the channel to avoid the irritative news from the reporters, and the general who was about to speak. She looked at the bathroom door, wondering if she was making a deadly mistake. "He's not dangerous. He really needs my help," were the thoughts speaking in her brain. It wasn't long before the bathroom door unlocked and cracked open. Marcus poked his head out. "Angel, didn't you say you had some clothes for me," asked Marcus, reminding her. "Oh yeah! I'm sorry Marcus. One moment," she replied.

Angel hopped out of the bed and headed for her closet. She still had alot of her deceased husband's clothing hanging up. She wanted to keep them close, for good memories. Besides, she hadn't moved on, and wasn't quite ready to let go. She grabbed a nice pair of Levi jeans, and a polo shirt for Marcus. Angel closed the closet back and took the clothing over to the bathroom. She politely knocked on her bathroom door, and Marcus opened the door. He reached out, grabbed the clothes, and said, "Thanks Angel."

⇨ Tina, Taran, Draggono, Rebel, and the other pterodactyls and raptors, were spying on the bank. The Manosaurs were lurking outside of the bank, in human form. They didn't need firearms, because they were just as dangerous. They didn't fear being shot by a firearm either. Taran orchestrated the whole criminal episode. He gave his instructions to the other 14 Manosaurs. He spoke to Rebel and the other 6 raptors first.

"Rebel! You and the raptors go inside and make everyone get on the ground. Do not kill anybody until we get the vault open. I would be extremely upset if we kill the only human, who knows the combination to the vault, understood?," said Taran, aggressively. The 7 Manosaurs nodded. Although the three females looked beautiful they would fool a person. They were the most vicious, and fearless of the Manosaurs. They were so bold, that they even had the audacity to disrespect Tarantulasaurus at times. Taran looked at Tina, and the 5 Manosaur's along the side of her.

"Tina! You and the pterodactyls watch for any ambush. I am sure they'll at least be one or two security guards with guns inside the bank. If they pull a gun, annihilate them immediately. Once Rebel gets the vault open, bag up all the money. Then you and the pterodactyls fly it to the secret hiding place!, Understood?" said Taran, seriously.

"We got it," replied Tina. "I know many cops will come! I know they will bring their fancy guns, and try to kill us. That's the reason why I want us to take every dollar inside of that bank. Me and Draggono will be outside waiting on the police officers to come. Don't worry about them! Take as much time as you need. We will handle the humans with the big guns," said Taran, seriously. Rebel spoke up and gave his opinion. "Taran! You should come in and rip the vault open," said Rebel. "Absolutely not! I can't leave Draggono out here alone to fight the police with guns. If he is outnumbered, and they over throw him, then we all will be killed. Besides, if I transform into my dinosaur form inside of that bank, the whole place will collapse. Draggono and I are too tall to stand up in that place," said Taran, intelligently.

The Manosaur had already mastered the plan like the architect. Taran was very brilliant Manosaur and diagramed things meticulously. "I see exactly what you mean now," said Rebel. "Just follow my instructions and everything shall go well," said Taran, smiling. Draggono was silently listening. Although he was mainly focused on obtaining a full moon stone, he was attentive to the masterplan. Robbing a bank was minutiae to him. Without any further elaboration, the Manosaurs began moving into their required formation. Taran and Draggono remained outside of the bank watching their protégés, go to work. The first seven Manosaurs transformed into raptors and entered violently.

The 6 pterodactyls flew in right behind them. You could hear screaming and cries for help, as soon as the 13 dinosaurs rushed into the establishment. It was apparent the creatures were not in the bank for depositing, withdrawing, or borrowing money. Rebel was the leader and spokesman, for the group of dangerous robbing reptiles. He slapped a woman in the face with his powerful claws. The woman flew sideways behind the counter. Rebel jumped off the counter onto the floor where she was. The lady cried, terrorfied her life was about to come to a end. The reptile looked into her pretty green eyes and spoke.

"Open the vault and I will let you live!," said the 10 foot tall Raptor. The lady was trembling with fear, as she pointed in the direction behind Rebel. "Only he can open the vault," she said, crying heavily. The vicious raptor glanced behind him. He saw the man she was referring too. The man was being held hostage in a corner by the other raptors and pterodactyls, just like every human in the bank was. Rebel pointed at the man. "You! Come over here and open the vault! Or I will eat you alive!," shouted Rebel the Raptor. The man knew Rebel was talking to him because he was the manager, and the only one who could open the vault.

He hurried over to meet the reptiles demand because he feared the threat. Rebel followed the man through a door into the back of the bank. As they went to the back, two security guards emerged from somewhere, and began shooting their glocks at the dinosaurs. The armed guards both managed to shoot a few of the raptors and pterodactyls, but the creatures didn't die. They were much stronger than a human, and bullets to the body would not kill them. Unless they were severely shot in the heart or the head, the Manosaurs would only become angrier. However, that is what happened.

Tina the Pterodactyl, and Rebecca the Raptor attacked the two guards like bolts of lightning. With no remorse, the female, reptilians ripped the humans apart, teaching them a valuable, deadly lesson. Blood covered the floor of the clean bank, and dripped from the jaws of the two female Manosaurs. "Tina! I am going back there to see what's taking King Rebel so long," said Rebecca the raptor. As the 7-foot-tall female raced toward the back room of the bank, loud noises erupted from outside of the bank! It sounded like cars being blown up and dinosaurs were angry because of the roaring.

Outside of the bank, dozens of police cars were approaching quickly. Red, white and blue lights were flashing rapidly on top of the police cars, as they rushed toward the bank. Draggonosaurus stood 23-foot-tall, in the middle of the road, spitting gigantic fire balls at the squad cars. As the huge balls of fire went flying through the air towards the police vehicles, officers inside had no time to exit. The police cars were blowing up back to back, and being totally destroyed by Draggonosaurus.

The 22 foot tall, all black dinosaur stood a few yards away from him, assisting him destructively. The Tarantulasaurus was just as mean, or worst. As a helicopter hovered above them and began shooting fully automatic machine guns at the two of them, the gigantic dinosaurs began roaring very loudly. The Tarantulasaurus looked up at the helicopter and released a very thick and long string of sticky spider web at the aircraft. The sticky web shook the helicopter, and stuck to it like glue on impact. Tarantulasaurus yanked the sticky spider web, and the helicopter came crashing down to the ground. The aircraft blew up instantly as it hit the ground.

The big explosion caused black smoke to linger in the air. The black dinosaur was the angriest. He immediately began shooting spider web out of his mouth and tail. The Tarantulasaurus started yanking cars and slinging them in all types of directions. Some of the police cars went flying through the air crashing into buildings.

Draggonosaurus and Tarantulasaurus were a dominant, destructive, dinosaur duo. The two creatures prevented all the police from arriving to the bank, and stopping the robbery. The two monstrous Manosaurs annihilated every single squad car in the vicinity, within minutes. They did not cease their disruption and destruction, until they saw 6 pterodactyls flying out of the bank with huge bags filled with money.

Each flying reptile had two big bags of money. One bag in each of their claws they usually walked on. Rebel, and Rebecca the raptor, came out quickly with bags of money also. The other 5 raptors came out viciously behind the two of them.

"Were ready Taran! Let's go!" shouted Rebel. The 9 dinosaurs stomped away on foot, following the pterodactyls in the air.

CHAPTER 9

Falling in Love with a Manosaur

It was 12:58 p.m., and Dr. Gladstone was still at the Cancer Treatment Center in Carson City. He had been there 6 hours, patiently waiting to see if the cancer would continue to eradicate the cancer, out of the two children like it had begun to do. The two kids were identical, 6 year old twins. A precious little girl named Americah, and her brother named Dillan. The kid's parents had signed waivers and gave the doctors consent to test the cure on their children. Regardless, of the side effects, the doctors and treatment center would not be held responsible for any mishaps. Dr. Gladstone looked down at his antique Rolex to see what time it was. He noticed the time was almost 1:00 p.m. precisely. He was watching the time to make sure he checked up on the two kids he had injected with Marcus blood. Every two hours, Dr. Gladstone and Dr. Tulip would go evaluate the amount of cancer that was eradicated.

"Dr. Tulip! Come on! We need to go check on the children again. It's that time of hour," said Dr. Gladstone. Dr. Tulip stopped his studies to go assist his colleague. They both were beyond interested in the discovery that was found in Marcus D.N.A. The two doctors were entering the lab within a half minute. They approached the beds, examined the machines, and monitors, that were attached to the children. The advanced technology was detecting the cancer, and automatically revealed to the doctors the status of the cancer, inside the human body. The two doctors stood side-by-side, analyzing the computer screen.

"Oh my Dr. Tulip! 25.8 percent of the cancer has been wiped out of Americah's body!," said Dr. Gladstone, surprised. They both noticed the dramatic change and were amazed. "I've been a physician for 43 years, and I never seen nothing like this," said Dr. Tulip, astonished. The old doctor rubbed his gray and white hair on top of his head. "It's exterminating the cancer 4.3 percent an hour! This is really amazing. The molecules in this rare blood is really preventing the tissue from growing. It's like …. it has taken control of the cellular proliferation, and attacking the tumors," said Dr. Gladstone, analyzing the children.

The two twins were in deep sleep while the potential cure for cancer was being tested on them. The twins had been suffering for years with it. They had been battling the malignant evil disease for 141 weeks now.

Since then, the cancer had continuously spreaded destructively through their small, innocent little bodies. "It's only been 6 hours! If the molecules in the blood continues to fight the cancer at this rate, within 24 hours, it may be eradicated completely," said the old Dr. Tulip, intelligently.

"This is truly unbelievable! It has really stopped the cancer from running, or moving to another location. I mean …. it's like it is surrounding it and … Oh my God … It's the cure Dr. Tulip! His blood! I think it's the cure for cancer," said Dr. Gladstone, stuttering. He was so excited and overwhelmed that he couldn't speak correctly.

⇨ Angel and Marcus were in her room being very open and friendly. The two of them laughed, told jokes, and reminisced on their past. Angel told him about the car crash she was in with her husband and 6-year-old son. She gave Marcus precise details of the incident and how she was the only one to manage to survive. She told him about her life as a heart surgeon, and how she had saved so many lives in Las Vegas.

Marcus did the same. He told Angel the story of how his father and brother were killed in Las Ventures. He told her all about the three past wars of the Manosaurs. He told her about Frogasaurus, Turtlesaurus, Tarantulasaurus, and Draggonosaurus. Although Marcus was born a Manosaur, he told her the same story his father and mother told him of how they were transmogrified into Manosaurs. Angel listened carefully giving Marcus her undivided attention. His life story was extremely interesting to her. They had no idea the time was 5:00 in the afternoon. Time was flying by so fast, as the two associates grew to learn alot about one another, in such little time.

"Wow! It's like you were living in a whole other galaxy!," she said, excitedly. The two were both sitting in her bed, relaxing. "Yeah! Las Ventures was a beautiful place until December 12th," he said, sadly. "Yeah I feel your pain. I wish I could have at least visited the place one time with you. I ... mean .... I never knew there were other dinosaurs like Frogasaurus, Turtlesaurus, Draggonosaurus, Tarantulasaurus, and Albinosaurus. I can't even imagine what they would look like," said Angel, honestly.

Marcus laughed. "You know what! You haven't even told me what kind of dinosaur you are deep down inside," said Angel, curiously. "Well Angel I am Megasaurus," he said. She was confused by the new name. "You're a what!," she said shocked. "I am a Megasaurus. It's a mixture of a Tyrannosaurus which was my father, and the extremely rare Albinosaurus, which was my mother. I am the first of my kind," said Marcus, truthfully. "Wow! And what about your daughter, was she a Megasaurus also?," she asked, curiously.

"No! She came out just like her mother. A full blood Tyrannosaurus. I have no idea why the DNA works so mysteriously," he said. The two were startled by a knock on the door. The person even tried to turn the door knob, and enter the room, but the door was locked. Since the door was locked, the child knocked harder. "Mommy! Can we come out of our rooms? Please!," shouted Abagail, loudly.

"Yes you may Abbie! Seems to me! You've already came out of your room," shouted Angel. "Mommy open this door! Who is that man you have in there?," shouted Abagail. "Abbie! Go away!," shouted Angel, blushing. "Mommy! Are you cheating on dad?," asked Abagail, trying to spoil their fun. Angel jolted out of the bed, ran to the door, and snatched it open! "Abagail! You need to stop it right now! Your father is dead! Please don't start with me," shouted Angel. Abagail stared in her mother's eyes for a moment, then turned, and walked away. Angel took a deep breath, then closed the door back. She locked it also, to avoid Abagail barging in and awkwardly interrupting her romanticizing. She hurried back to the bedroom and said, "Kids! Can't live with them, or without them."

Marcus wasn't listening to anything she was saying. She noticed the television had captivated Marcus undivided attention. "Oh my God! Another dinosaur attack," shouted Angel. She quickly grabbed the remote control to the huge flat screen television, and raised the volume up. Marcus knew every every single manosaur that was on television robbing the bank. All the raptors and pterodactyls looked similar to one another, from a normal human's eye. However, Marcus could determine the difference between each individual manosaur instantly.

He saw Draggonosaurus spitting gigantic fireballs, eradicating police cars, and blowing them up. The police men never even got the opportunity to exit their vehicles.

The fireballs came flying at their cars from hundreds of feet away. Tarantulasaurus was right in the middle of the road with Draggono. It was all caught on video footage. Marcus and Angel were seeing it for themselves.

The huge, black, 4 legged, 4 arm dinosaur was slinging his long tail, and shooting sticky spider web out his mouth and his tail. He was yanking the police cars off the ground into the air. He would crush them with his jaws, or just send them crashing into some random building. A helicopter hovered above them and began firing rapid shots at the two, 20-foot-tall reptiles. In less than thirty seconds, it was a victim of their destruction also.

Angel looked at Marcus horrified, worried, and scared a little. "Marcus! Please tell me you are nothing like those animals," said Angel, concerned. Marcus stood up and took a deep breath. "I am not Angel! Can't you see that I am different and humble," he said, shyly. "Do you know those dinosaurs? Are they your friends and family?," she asked. "Yes and No!" he replied, in order. "Yes! No! What the hell does that mean Marcus?," she said, afraid. "I know every Manosaur Angel! But No! They are my enemies! Not my friends! And most certainly not my family," he said, angrily.

"I didn't mean to offend you Marcus," said Angel. "Angel I have to go! I must find my family and friend before those wicked manosaurs do," he said, seriously. Marcus began walking towards the bedroom door. Angel hopped out of bed and shouted. "No Marcus! Please don't go!" "Listen Angel! I am the King of the Manosaurus! My species need me! I can't just abandon them and hide in this house like some coward," he said.

Angel stood in front of the door blocking the exit. "I don't want anything to happen to you Marcus! I haven't met a nice man like you in a long time. Just please don't leave me! When my children go to school tomorrow, I will help you find your family and friends. I will promise," she assured him. "How can you be so certain we will find them?," he asked, curiously. "Because Marcus. I am a doctor. I know a lot of ways of finding out things. Now please! Stay put. I have to go cook dinner for my kids. I didn't realize it was this late," she said, seriously.

"Okay Angel. I will be patient. She looked into his eyes and showing him she was genuinely attracted to him by looking seductive at him. She used one finger to pull her hair behind her right ear. She moved forward towards Marcus, looking deeply into the eyes of the unusual human. He stepped forward also, and the two of them began tongue kissing. The two kissed passionately, like they were infatuated with one another. After they slowly stopped kissing, Angel smiled. "It's been awhile since I've done that," she said.

"Don't you think we're moving too fast. I mean, we just met yesterday," said Marcus, informing her. "Hold up Marcus! To be exact, I met you 3 months ago at the hospital. Not yesterday! Besides, after all we've talked about over the last 8 hours, I feel like I've known you forever," said Angel, seriously. "I understand Angel. But I was always taught to be very careful. You could catch a disease, and get sick," he replied. "I am a doctor Marcus! I am as clean as bleach! If you know what that is. And as for you, you are clean to," she said. "I am a Manosaur. I am half dinosaur. How can you be so sure?" he asked.

"Maybe because I tested your blood myself while you were in the hospital in a coma," she said, smiling. Angel winked her eye at Marcus and walked out of the bedroom. She knew Abagail was going to be impudent and sassier than ever before. However, Angel was ready to be the sassiest female in the house, and show Abbie, she could be impertinent also.

⇨ Rebel, Taran, and Draggono sat in the living room area counting the money. The 6 females in the mansion were surrounding them and assisting them. The time was 9:19 p.m., and the bad manosaurs had been counting millions of dollars for hours. The reptiles had taken more money than they'd expected to get. The 15 loyal manosaurs had committed the biggest bank robbery in history of America. Never had a group of 15 people committed a bank robbery mission together. Never had so many millions of dollars been taken from any bank during a robbery. The Manosaurs had remained in the bank 3 minutes and 16 seconds, without any firearms and manage to get almost every penny out of the place.

"Rebel! The ladies and I are hungry! We haven't ate anything all day," said Rebecca, honestly. Rebel looked at her. "What! Why didn't you all eat some of those humans at the bank," he replied. "Because Taran order us not to! He didn't want us killing the wrong person who could possibly open the vault," shouted Rebecca, hostily. Taran and Draggono looked at the spokesperson for the women. "She's right Rebel. Those were my specific orders," said Taran seriously.

Rebel shouted! "Dammit! It's almost 9:30 at night! The damn moon is out," he replied. "Rebel we are grown women! Quit trying to control us and treat us like children," shouted Tonya, the pterodactyl. The ladies were still in their human form inside the mansion. When Tonya spoke up, her voice was always respected.

"You all go out and get you something to eat. Just be careful my love. That moon can cause you all to get carried away," said Taran, nicely. Taran was so in love with money and had accomplished his masterplan. He was happy and content. Tonya kissed Draggono, and before they knew it, the women exited the home. As the 6 women walked outside, and glanced up at the moon, they transformed into their dinosaur form. Three women turned into vicious female raptors! The other three began transforming and growing into vicious female pterodactyls.

It was obvious from the look in their eyes, faces and mouth, they were possessed. It was like the moon had a very evil effect on them. They were meaner, angrier, more aggressive than usual. The raptors took off running extremely fast with the 3 pterodactyls flying right above them. The 3 raptors were moving quicker than a cheetah could. They were drooling from their powerful jaws like they had rabies. They were ready to devour any human, any domestic animal, or wild animal, that came in their path. All 6 of them were on a hungry rampage, and ready to slaughter the first person or animal in their way.

⇨ The time was precisely 11:00 pm. when Dr. Gladstone entered into the lab where the two twins were. The two hairless children were wide awake, lying in the hospital beds, watching the doctor as he walked in. As he glanced at Dillan and Americah, he became sad all over again. He hated to see little children suffering from the cancer disease. Observing an innocent little girl practically hairless with very little strings on her head, bothered him alot. He approached the two 6-year-old twins with a genuine smile.

"How are you two feeling?" asked the doctor. "I feel okay," said Americah, smiling. "And what about you Dillan?" he asked. "I'm okay. Just hungry Doc," said Dillan. "Well its eleven, o'clock now. After I am done checking how potential the cure for cancer is doing, I will tell the nurses to bring extra food for you two," said Dr. Gladstone. "Can we have ice cream?" asked Americah, in her sweet little voice.

Dillan assisted her request. "Yeah Doc! Can we have ice cream?" He looked at both of them and said, "What do you say?" "Pleassssse," said Americah and her brother in unison. The two kids were smiling at the doctor, showing both of their pretty white teeth. The kids had orchestrated a request he couldn't refuse. "Okay kids! Ice cream will be added for desert." Said Dr. Gladstone, smiling. "Yay" said Americah, happily.

"Doc you're the best doctor ever," said Dillan. Dr. Gladstone walked over to the computers and laboratory experimental equipment. He began inspecting and evaluating the cancer in the children's tiny bodies. "Wow! It's still fighting of the cancer," he said to himself. He grabbed a small pad and pen out the pocket of his white lab coat. "68.8 percent," he whispered to himself, as he wrote it down. He looked at the kids and smiled, and placed the utensils back in his pocket. "Well doc, what do you see," asked Dillan intelligently.

"I see progress kids. I must call your parents and tell them the good news," he said. "Tell us first Doc," shouted Dillan. "Yeah Doc! Tell us what's going on. We want to know," said Americah, sincerely. Dr. Gladstone was hesitant and deliberated mentally before revealing his findings. Dr. Gladstone gave his explanation to them. "Well the things in his blood seems to be killing the cancer. It has got rid of seventy percent of it out of your body for good," said the doctor.

"Really!" exclaimed Americah, astonished. "Yes kiddo! You two are probably going to owe me and God a big thank you," he said. "How much longer do you think it will take before the cancer goes bye bye forever?," asked the 6 year old girl, innocently. "Well it's only been 16 hours and 68 percent of the cancer has gone away. So according to the machine approximately 8 more hours, if the cure continues attacking the cancer at the same pace it has been," he said. "Mommy said its 24 hours in one day. So 8 hours is less than one day," said Dillan aware.

"Yes Dillan! 8 hours is tomorrow," said the Doctor. "Tomorrow! That's amazing," said Americah, surprised. "Yeah, that really is amazing! Isn't it," said Doc. "Yeah! Now me and Dillan will be normal like the rest of the kids. Right Doc?," said Americah, happily. "Yes sweet heart. That's right," replied Dr. Gladstone, proudly. "Do you think my hair will grow long and pretty now?," asked Americah curiously. Although Dr. Gladstone was unsure, he decided to inspire, and motivate the pretty little blonde hair child. "Of course Americah! But when your hair gets long and pretty, don't go taking all the girls boyfriends," he said smiling. She couldn't help but smile.

"I won't take all of them doc. I promise," she replied. "Okay kiddo. That's a good girl," he replied. Americah didn't feel pretty knowing she was bald head. Her hair didn't grow long and pretty like the other girls, which made her feel ashamed and ugly. After Dr. Gladstone informed her that she would be a normal kid in a few more hours, her outlook on life changed. She felt alive. She felt special. She felt like she could be somebody, or anything she wanted to be in life now.

"Alright you two, relax and wait patiently. I'll be back to check on you in a few hours," said Dr. Gladstone. "Me too" said Dr. Macin well. "Okay doc's," said the boy.

As the doctors walked away toward the door of the room Americah spoke. "Doc - wait!," shouted Americah. The doctor looked back and asked, "What is it Americah?" "Don't forget the ice cream," she said smiling. Dr. Gladstone gave the kids a thumbs up, and winked at them. "Gotcha! Ice cream on the way," he replied. The two twins smiled. "You're the best doctor in the world," said Dillan.

Before he exited the lab room he said, "I hope so kid." He walked out of the lab, and closed the door. He looked up at the ceiling. "God knows if this is the cure for cancer, I will be kid. I most certainly will be," whispered Dr. Gladstone, to himself.

⇨ Angel and Marcus were laying in the bed together. Although Angel wanted to have sex, she was contemplating on how to go about it. She hadn't laid with a man since her husband had died, almost a year ago. With no other way to start a conversation, she brought up Teresa's mother. "Marcus what was Teresa's mother like?" she asked. Marcus glanced over at Angel. He was sitting on top of the blankets, watching the television. Although he had no idea how the electronic showed show many different motion pictures, it taught him alot of things very quickly, by watching it.

"Teresa's mother was the loveliest manosaur to ever live in Las Ventures," he replied. Marcus continued eyeballing the huge flat screen. Angel was laughing underneath the sheets and blankets in her silk lingerie. "What was her name Marcus? If you don't mind me asking?," said Angel, keeping the conversation alive. "Annebella," he replied. "That's a beautiful name. I like the sound of that," said Angel smiling.

"Thank you. Angel is a very beautiful name!" "Well thanks Marcus," she replied. "Your name fits you Angel. You have a beautiful soul, and you're a nice person. I thank God I ran into you, and not some manosaur hunter," said Marcus, seriously. Angel smiled. "Awe Marcus! That's so sweet," she replied. She reached over and placed her hands on his. The manosaur looked over and made eye contact with her. Angel gave him a seductive look that made him interested in her. Too long of staring, made them start kissing. The two of them tongue kissed like they were in love, and missed each other. Although they'd never been intimate with each other, they were on the road to do it.

Angel spoke up and said, "Marcus I haven't had sex in almost a year! I am going to lose my mind if I don't find a man quicker than tomorrow." "Look at me Angel! You have one right here," said Marcus. He took off his shirt and got up under the covers. The two continued kissing and it lead to something more.

CHAPTER 10

Reuniting with Megasaur!

Marcus was lying in bed asleep when Angel woke up at 6:16 a.m. She glanced over at the man of her dreams and smiled. Angel got out of the bed, took a quick shower, then got dressed. When she went downstairs to cook breakfast, Abagail, was in the living room sitting on the couch. Angel paused for a moment. When Abbie looked up at her, she walked toward her daughter, and sat on the sofa beside her. "What's the matter Abbie?"

"Nothing Mommy. I'm fine. It's just, Anthony and I don't like you keeping secrets from us. If you're trying to make us have a new daddy, you have to at least let us meet him to see if we like him too," said the 10 year old, intelligently. Angel was moved by the statement. She grabbed Abagail and embraced her.

"Awe Abbie. I am not trying to make you two have a new daddy. No man in this world can ever replace your father sweetie," said Angel, sadly. Abagail smiled and said "really!"

"Yes really honey! Now Marcus is a very nice person. And I really like him alot. But I wanted to get to know him first, before I let you guys meet him," she said. "So if he's a nice guy can we meet him?," asked Abagail, excited. Angel glanced upstairs thinking about the Manosaur in her bedroom. "Maybe some other time. Alright baby," said Angel.

"Okay Mommy. It's just things haven't been the same since dad died. And Anthony and I need another parent to talk to sometimes. You are too busy for us sometimes," said Abagail, honestly. "No I don't!" "You do too mommy!"

"Well I guess I am going to have to look into that. And if that's true, I'm going to stop being so busy, and spend more time talking with you two," said Angel. "Thanks Mom! That'll really be nice," said Abagail. "Well let me go cook you guys a nice breakfast before I take you to school." "Can we just by McDonalds on the way to school?," asked Abagail, quickly. "Yeah. I guess we can just do that," replied Angel, smiling. Angel went upstairs, and told Marcus to stay put. She informed him she was going to go take the kids to school, and that she'd be right back. Marcus looked in Angel's eyes.

"And will you help me find my friends and family when you return?," asked Marcus, genuinely concerned about the other Manosaurs. Without hesitation, she replied "Yes Marcus. Soon as I get back we will start searching for them," said Angel. She quickly gave Marcus a kiss on the lips. The half man, half dinosaur, was still lying in the bed in his underclothes, as Angel exited the bedroom.

Angel and the two children exited the front door of their residence, and headed for the Mercedes Benz. The family entered inside the white luxurious vehicle, and departed. They had a very personal conversation about their family priorities during the car ride. They all compromised, came to a better understanding, and agreed on better communication with one another.

They made a quick stop by the McDonald's fast food restaurant. Angel ordered the children whatever they asked for, and waited for the food to be served by the drive thru personnel. As Angel reached out to grab the brown bags filled with breakfast, the lady in the white shirt said, "Thank you for coming to McDonalds." Angel nodded her head, handed the food to her son in the passenger seat, and pressed on the gas pedal. The white Mercedes Benz departed the restaurant and headed towards the private school. The two children gobbled down the delicious and tasty breakfast, while their motherly chauffeur took them to their destination.

It wasn't long before they arrived to the private school that was expensive. Angel gave each of her kids a kiss, and told them she loved them as they exited the Benz. "See you later mommy," said Abagail, smiling and waving. Angel blew her young princess a kiss, and waved bye bye to her. Angel watched as the two children with backpacks on their backs, entered into the school. Once they walked all the way inside, Angel departed. As she was leaving out of the school premises, her cellular phone rang. Angel looked to the screen and saw it was Dr. Gladstone. She answered her phone respectfully.

"Hello there Dr. Gladstone," she said, already knowing who was calling. "Hey Dr. Nixon. I have some great news," he said happily. "Go ahead. I am listening," replied Angel, attentively. "That blood was the cure! His DNA attacked the tumors, ceased the tissue from growing and decreased the proliferation of the cancer cells!" said Dr. Gladstone. "Jesus Christ doc! That's great! Who did you test it on?," she asked.

"You're not going to believe it. Two 6-year-old twins! I injected the blood in them yesterday morning. Now the cancer is completely gone," he said, excitedly. "Are you serious? That's incredible," she replied, happily. "By the way we must find this guy! Did you manage to get his full name before he left the hospital," asked Dr. Gladstone, curiously.

"No doc! All I k now is his first name is Marcus," she said, dishonestly. The doctor contemplated before replying. "Well I'm going to recheck the database and try to narrow it down. Hopefully his first name, blood type, race, and age range will help me find a possible name," said the doctor. "I don't know doc. That sounds kind of farfetched. You're going to need a last name and date of birth," said Angel, honestly.

"Well Angel we have to find this man again. He holds the cure for cancer. And it may sound preposterous. But even if I have to pay hundreds of millions of dollars, I will find him!," said Dr. Gladstone, very serious.

Angel knew the Doctor was wealthy and really had the money, to do exactly that. She also knew any business man would do the same, knowing the astronomical amount of money it would bring back to him in the end. "Well doc I wish you luck! If I get any information concerning that patient again, I will be sure to contact you right away," said Angel untruthfully.

"Okay Angel. Please do so," he replied, as he ended the phone call. Angel was astonished by the new information. As she drove her car she thought about Marcus. "He doesn't even know. He has no idea his blood is a cure for cancer." she thought, mentally. After more meditation and consideration.

"He could easily become a billionaire over night! This would easily make him one of the richest people in the world," she thought. Angel smiled to herself. As she drove a few miles over the speed limit, she arrived back home quicker than usual. She drove the white Benz into the driveway of her nice two-story home, and parked it.

The sophisticated heart surgeon grabbed her purse, exited the vehicle, and hurried into the home.

Marcus was there waiting for her to return. He was seated at the dining table meditating patiently. He stood up as she entered. "Is everything alright Angel?," asked Marcus, concerned. She tried to hide her feelings. "Oh yes. Yes Marcus. Everything is fine! Why?," she asked? "Because Angel ... I sense something within you. You're hiding something from me," said the manosaur. Angel's facial expression showed confusion.

"Why do you say such a thing?," "Listen Angel. Once a manosaur becomes intimate with a woman, we can sense strong emotions, and energy from the other person. My gut instincts is tingling. You can't fool me Angel," said Marcus, seriously. "Okay Marcus! There are a couple things I need to tell you. While you were in the hospital doctors did test on your blood, they found something in your blood that has never been found in anyone's blood on Earth," she said.

She paused and thought. "And what is that?" asked Marcus. "A cure for a disease called cancer. Your blood has some very powerful molecules that attack the tumors, stops the evil disease from spreading, and reproducing rapidly in the human body! We have no cure for this disease, and millions of people are dying from it Marcus! With your blood and your help we could save millions of little children that are dying daily, from this disease," said Angel, seriously. Marcus was silent, as he thought about her word.

"Angel you humans are so concerned with finding remedies, and antidotes to save lives and become rich. We are born to die! Everybody's dying to live for longer number of years, but it's inevitable! We are living to die. Some diseases and plagues are not to be cured. For some of them are sent by the creator of this earth. Whoever has been lucky enough, and blessed to be cured by the blood that has already been stolen from me, that was God's plan. But Angel, I do not wish to be some experiment for humans to conquer kingdoms, and get wealthy off of," said Marcus, honestly.

Angel walked over and placed her expensive purse on the dining room table "Okay Marcus. That's your prerogative! I was just telling you," she said, not happy with his words. "Maybe after I help my family and friends, I can consider helping others. But until then, you are the only human I trust to get close to me. I'll rip anyone else apart angel," said Marcus seriously.

Angel grabbed her laptop and sat the computer down on the table. She sat down at the front of the computer. "Rip anyone else apart huh Marcus! You told me you were humble and not like those animals we saw on T.V. yesterday!," she shouted angrily. The manosaur was silent and did not reply at all. He had put his foot in his mouth, metaphorically speaking. She glanced up and looked into the red pupils of the unique human. "Marcus I really like you alot. You have become something special to me in such a little time. I want you to be a part of my family but I know we are two different kind of humans. The only thing I fear is you turning into some dinosaur that goes on a rampage, and start killing people," she said, seriously.

"That's not who I am Angel" replied Marcus. "And I believe that to be true that's why I trust you," she said. Angel continued scanning on her computer, and typing in words. "Oh and by the way! This is the thing we call the computer, that has the internet," said Angel smiling! She knew that would mess with his head. She knew he would be surprised about the technological information. "What! That's the thing we call the computer and knows everything in the world?," he said, greatly astonished. Angel laughed at his astonishment.

"Yes Marcus! This is the thing that tells us anything we want to know," she said chuckling. Marcus had moved closer to the computer to examine the screen. The manosaur's eyes inspected every inch of the screen precisely, with his red pupils. Although the manosaur was intelligent to learning, understanding, and sharp he wasn't smart on new technology. "So this will help us find my family and friends," said Marcus, unsure. If your Manosaurs have turned into dinosaurs and did something in Las Vegas, it will be on here. If they were caught, or found anywhere, we will know exactly, what happened, and where it happened at. What I need for you to do is, tell me if you see any of your family in any of these attacks by Manosaurs. Because there has been alot of attacks," said Angel "But Angel, my friends and family are not bad and mean. They don't cause destruction and try to harm people," said Marcus, honestly.

Angel looked at him like he was lying and untrustworthy. "What Angel! Don't look at me that way! I'm serious! My friends are herbivores," he said "You told me your family was tyrannosauruses, I've heard of that dinosaur. And I think it's a carnivore that eats flesh, not a herbivore," said Angel, with knowledge. "Yes your right! But all of my friends are herbivores and plant eaters! All of my family of Tyrannosauruses are dead, except one. My grandson Little Rex. He's the only real family I have left. He's the most important person and my life Angel. He's the manosaur I miss the most, and need to find," said Marcus, extremely emotional. Angel could see the sadness and worries in Marcus's facial expression. His pain kind of rubbed off on her, and she felt concerned.

"Don't worry Marcus. We will find little Rex, and your friends. Let's just do our researching," she said, softly. Angel continued typing in all sorts of things about Manosaurs. Several different things were popping up. Florence McKinley had shocked the world 3 months ago with her live video down in Las Ventures. After the Archaeologist went viral, the whole world became interested in the discovery of the manosaurs. It was amazing how many people had uploaded strange things to the world wide web.

After Florence had proved the manosaurs were living creatures. There was a book, a film, a t.v. series and a video game for children, and teenagers, about the manosaurs, and their unique transformations.

"Wow! There is so many new things about your species Marcus," said Angel, as she googled the word: Manosaurs. Many attacks had happened all over the world over the past years. However, the newest attacks were right in Las Vegas. "Look Marcus! Do you know any of these Manosaurs?," asked Angel, astonished by the creatures. "Yes I know each and every last one of them," he said honestly.

Angel pointed at the screen. "Which is he? He looks very mean and dangerous," she said sincerely. She was pointing at the black dinosaur with 8 limbs. "That is Tarantulasaurus! He is the master of destruction." "And what about that one? He looks mean also," said Angel. She was pointing at the reddish, pink skinned dinosaur. "That's Draggonosaurus in particular."

"Looks like he spits fire out of his mouth in that picture. Raptors don't spit fire and they're not as tall as him! Are you sure he's half and half?" She asked. "Angel I know my species like you know black humans from a white human, or a Chinese human. Draggonosaurus gets the height from our mother, the Albinosaurus. Also, the rare and unique bloodline of Albinosaurus, gives him the ability to spit fireballs." "You said our mother! This is your brother?" she asked shocked. Marcus hesitated to claim the bad dinosaur as a part of his family. "Unfortunately yes. We have the same mother and different fathers," said Marcus.

"So you can spit fire too," said Angel, smiling like it was cool. She was ready to see him spit fire if he could. "No Angel! The blood line of Albinosaurus is weird! I have a huge sharp curved horn on my forehead when I transform into a Megasaurus. But no Tyrannosaurus or Albinosaurus has that. Coincidentally, the

Draggonosaurus is the first and only manosaur I know of, that can spit fire," said Marcus, sincerely.

After he was done speaking, she looked back at the computer. Angel continued scrolling through the internet looking at recent dinosaur attacks by manosaurs in Las Vegas. "Stop!", shouted Marcus, extremely loud. "What Marcus! What is it?," she asked, afraid. The manosaur had scared her immediately "Wait! Go back!," said Marcus seriously. Angel used her finger to back-track, and move backwards to the images she had just passed. She continued scrolling in reverse until Marcus said, "Hold it right there!" The manasaur had very sharp vision and didn't miss any details. His red pupils were like eagle eyes. He could spot an ant when he was standing 25 feet tall. "Where is that farm located?," he asked. "Why? What do you see so special about that farm in this picture," asked Angel, confused. "That bull! He has three huge holes in him," said Marcus alert. "So what! It looks like he was stabbed, three times with a sharp pole," she said. "No Angel! A Triceratops did that! I know the Mark of a triceratops when it rams another creature. I've seen it over a thousand times," said Marcus. He was very vigilant and nimble manosaur. Rarely did he miss anything, or forgot anything, that happened right in front of him. "So what! That could be any triceratops," said Angel. "No Angel! A baby triceratops did that. And only two triceratops managed to escape Las Ventures. Please find out where that farm is! We must go there immediately," said Marcus anxiously.

Angel did more research on the farm and its location. She got the address, then examined the article. As she was reading the article, Marcus spoke. "What does it say?," asked the manosaur. "The video will not play for me! But it says a camera near the barn caught video footage of a baby Tyrannosaurus slaughtering a cow. It also says a baby triceratops helped the baby tyrannosaurus, by ramming the bull in its side, as it charged over to help the cow," said Angel, as she inspected the article. "Chyna and Little Rex!" whispered Marcus. The manosaur smiled a little as his faith and hopes of reuniting with them rose highly. "Do you have the address of where that farm is located?" said Marcus. "Yes Marcus. I have it," she said. "Then we must go there! I must search that area," said Marcus.

⇨Americah and Dillan were both being held by their parents. Americah was in her mother's arms, and Dillan in his father's arms. The two 6 year olds felt better than ever. They were filled with happiness, and it was very obvious. The kids looked better and felt better than ever.

"Thank you so much Dr. Gladstone! There is nothing in this world we can do to repay you. And no amount of money, or words, can express how we feel to know our children are cancer free," said the father of the twins. "Yes it is daddy! A million gazillion bucks," shouted the 6 year old girl. The parents and Dr. Gladstone laughed at her childish comment. "I don't know how much a gazillion bucks is! But it sure sounds like a nice amount of money," said Dr. Gladstone, smiling.

The mother spoke as she held her 6-year-old daughter closely. "Dr. Gladstone. So if this cure for cancer going to be available for other children suffering around the world?," asked the mother. Dr. Gladstone glanced around at the other doctors and nurses who were listening to their conversation. Although they were not trying to look suspicious, it was obvious they were listening attentively.

"Well your children were the two luckiest kids in the world to be tested with the cure first. We have to find the source again, because we are unable to duplicate it. The cure must come directly from the source in order for us to cure more patients with cancer," said Dr. Gladstone, truthfully. He and a few other doctors had tried to duplicate the ingredients, and molecules in Marcus DNA. They had diligently tried every alternative there was to make a cure identical to Marcus blood, but was unsuccessful. "Well Dr. Gladstone we have to get going. Thanks a billion, and we will always keep in contact with you," said the mother.

"Tell the doctor thank you kids," said the father. "Thank you Dr. Gladstone," said Dillan, plainly. "You're welcome Dillan," he replied. "Thank you very, very, very, much, Dr. Gladstone," said Americah, smiling. "Awe! You are very, very, very welcome Americah," replied Dr. Gladstone, happily. The doctor watched as the two parents, and their set of twins departed. Americah waved goodbye to the doctor one last time, as her mother carried her out of the treatment center. Dr. Gladstone waved his last farewell to the pretty little considerate girl.

"Dr. Gladstone you look tired. You need to go home and get you some rest," said a female nurse. "Yeah you're right. I've been up over 24 hours now. I could use a little rest," he said. The Doctor, took a deep breath and rubbed his head. He covered his mouth as he started yawning. "Now I got to find this Marcus guy; where ever you are," he whispered to himself.

⇨ Philip and Brenda were standing outside of their 6-bedroom mansion in the woods. The two manosaurs were watching Rex and Chyna play together outdoors. After the incident at the barnyard, a couple hundred yards away, they decided to watch the 2 children at all times when they played outdoors. It was noon time when they saw a white car approaching their territory in the woods. Brenda spotted the car first.

"Humans!," she shouted, worried. Little Rex and Chyna were in their dinosaur form horseplaying. The two dinos weren't paying attention to their surroundings. Philip yelled loudly so the two baby manosaurs could hear him. "Little Rex! Chyna! Run," said Philip seriously. As the two dinos stomped away running toward the rear of the residence, Brenda followed. "Yes! Follow them Brenda! And don't let them out of your sight. I'll handle these humans!," shouted Philip angrily.

As the white Mercedes Benz drove toward the huge house in the woods, Philip began transforming, and growing into his Frogasaurus form. The huge green dinosaur stood 22-foot-tall ready to devour the humans in the car, and crush the vehicle also. As the white Mercedes drove closer to the residence that was deep in the forest, Frogasaurus discharged his long sticky tongue at the car. The car was tiny compared to the dinosaur. When the huge amphibious/reptile sticky tongue touched the car, it stuck like duct tape. Frogasaurus yanked the luxurious white car towards him. The $75,000 Sedan went flying towards the dinosaurs' huge mouth.

He had no idea Marcus was inside of the vehicle, until the car was closer. The Frogasaurus great eye sight caught a glimpse of Marcus in the Benz just about as the car was about to enter his powerful jaws, and be crushed by his huge teeth. He heard Marcus yell "Philip," at the same moment. The Frogasaurus grabbed the car with his sticky hands right off the end of his tongue as it was about to go into his mouth. The gigantic green manosaur looked into the Mercedes as he held it in his hand right in front of his face.

"Marcus", whispered the huge creature. "Yes Philip. It's me," said Marcus, from inside the car. Angel was terrified, and scared for her life. She had almost been eaten by some huge frog looking reptile, that had never been seen before. Angel was panicking in the driver seat, and almost had an anxiety attack. The green dinosaur placed the car back on the ground, where he had snatched it from. Angel was relieved as the Benz was put back on the forest grounds.

"Oh my God Marcus! I almost had a heart attack. I don't know how much more of this I can bear," said Angel, still trembling. "Everything's going to be okay," said Marcus, as he opened the car door. The Frogasaurus was shrinking down, and changing back to its human form. Timothy, Stoic, Stacey, and Tracey ran out of the house to see what was going on. As the Frogasaurus fully minimized into his human form, Philip walked over to Marcus. The two men hugged one another immediately. They embraced one another like they haven't seen each other in years. However, 3 months felt like forever. After they were done embracing one another, they talked.

"Marcus where have you been?," said Philip, very concerned. "I was in a coma for 3 months. But I've been searching for you all for the last 2 days," said Marcus. "Oh my God! It's Marcus!", shouted Tracey, excitedly. Marcus looked up and saw Tracey running towards him. He smiled, and gave her a big hug as she came close to him. Angel was still inside the car on the driver side. She felt a tingling feeling of jealousy as the female manosaur hugged the man she cares for. Tracey and Marcus hugged for about 7 seconds, without releasing one another.

"My God! It's great to see you again," she said. Stoic and Stacey walked up, gave Marcus a hug and embraced him also. It was like a manosaur reunion, as they welcomed their King of Las Ventures back again. Marcus glanced around. "Where's Brenda and little Rex?" asked Marcus, worried.

They are around back. We thought this white car were humans with guns coming to attack us. Paranoia has been a big issue for us lately," said Philip, truthfully. "I agree. For me too. Living in the real world with humans is quite different. But it's not difficult as expected," said Marcus. When Marcus looked to his left, he saw Brenda and the two children coming from behind the house. "Marcus! Is that really you?" said Brenda, astonished and shocked.

Little Rex was in his human form, and so was Chyna, when Rex saw Marcus, his eyes became very wide. The seven-year-old, unusual child, took off running towards his long lost grandfather. As he ran up to him, he yelled, "Pa-Pa! Pa-Pa!"

Marcus moved forward towards the 7-year-old manosaur coming his, and grabbed him. He picked up little Rex off of the ground and hugged the young child. "Rex! Thank God you're safe and okay," said Marcus, sadly. Tears rolled down the strong Manosaur's cheeks. He was crying tears of joy; tears of happiness, and tears of relief. Rex was smiling from ear to ear. He wasn't sad or teary at all. He looked in the red pupils of Marcus after they hugged.

"Pa-Pa! Why are you crying? You should be happy to see me! I'm happy to see you," said Rex, innocently. Marcus smiled and said, "I am happy Rex. I'm very happy to see you," said Marcus. Marcus looked over at Chyna and Brenda. "Hi King Megasaur," said Chyna nicely. "Come over here and give me a hug Chyna," he said.

The 6-year-old girl ran over and gave Marcus a hug. Marcus had both children in his arms now. He looked at his best friend Brenda, as she stood before him. The two close friends locked eyes as they stood face to face.

"Marcus where've you been? We thought you were dead!," said Brenda, seriously. "I've been in the hospital for 3 months. I was in a coma Brenda," he said. "How did you find us here?," asked Brenda. "Angel!" shouted Marcus, seriously. He had totally forgot about the woman that had assisted him with locating his friends and family. Marcus looked back at the white Mercedes Benz. He could see her through the window looking at him. Angel waved and mumbled to herself. "Oh now you remember me. I do think I deserved to be properly introduced to your dinosaur friends. After all, I did to help him find them", said Angel. She was inside the car talking to herself, so no one could hear her. She knew they were about to call her over and summon her out of the car.

Marcus made an announcement. "Manosaurs! I have someone I want you to meet. If it wasn't for her, I would be dead! And I would of never even found you at all," said Marcus loudly. "Who is Angel Pa-Pa?," asked Little Rex. Marcus put the two children down and motioned for Angel to get out of the car. "I think it's King Megasaur's new girlfriend," said Chyna smiling. "Chyna don't say that! She's a human. She can't be his girlfriend," said Tracey. Angel exited the white Benz and walked over to the crowd of nine manosaurs. Marcus introduced her to all of them.

Marcus pointed to each of them as he said their names. "Manosaurs this is Angel," said Marcus. Angel waved to all of them without saying a word. "And Angel, this is Timothy. This is Stoic, that's Stacey, that's Tracey and her daughter Chyna. That's Brenda, this is Philip. I believe you've already met him," said Marcus, smiling. Angel barely laughed. "God yes we were almost his lunch," she said. "Sorry Angel! I was only trying to protect my kind," said Philip, sincerely. "Trust me I understand. It's okay," replied Angel. After they concluded their short conversation, Rex spoke. "What about me Pa-Pa? You left me out! Tell Angel my name," said little Rex, anxiously.

Everybody smiled, because Marcus had really introduced everybody but little Rex. He had been temporarily interrupted from finishing his introduction, but he had no intentions of leaving out little Rex. "I would never leave you out Rex," Marcus looked at Angel quickly and said, "Angel this is my grandson I've been telling you about. Little Rex!" said Marcus, smiling. "Hello Angel. Nice to meet you," said Little

Rex, politely. "Nice to meet you too. Marcus has told me alot about you," said Angel, smiling.

"Bad stuff or good stuff!" Blurted out little Rex. All the Manosaurs, including Marcus and Angel began laughing at his comment. "I think all of it was good stuff," said Angel, assuring him.

⇨ Rebel the Raptor was in his dinosaur form standing in front of a computer. The 10-foot-tall manosaur was in the living room of the mansion alone. The other Manosaurs were in the dining room, and kitchen doing other things. Draggono walked into the living room and saw Rebel still searching on the internet for information. "Did you see or find anything of where those other manosaurs are hiding at?," asked Draggono.

Rebel clicked on a video, and it started playing for him. He saw the video of the baby tyrannosaurus slaughtering the cow. Then he saw a baby triceratops ram into a bull. "As a matter of fact. I think I just found where they are hiding out at," said the 10 foot tall Raptor.

Draggono was in his human form, so Rebel the Raptor was a few feet taller than him. He walked over, stood next to the reptile, and examined the computer with him. "Rewind that video again," said Draggono. Without hesitation, Rebel the Raptor replayed the video of the baby dinos at the farm. At the end of the video they saw Frogasaurus land in the barnyard. Unfortunately, there was only video and no audio. However, that was all the verification they needed. Draggono started grinning. "Rebel can you find the exact location of that farm in those woods?," asked Draggono. "I already have it my friend," said the vicious Raptor. "Excellent! Excellent! ... I guess it's time to get those full moon stones," said Draggono, wickedly. "Look Draggono! The 5 Tyrannosauruses and many other manosaurs have went to Europe and Africa." "Yes. I see! To a new land!"

To Be Continued ...

Manosaurs 2: Frogasaurus V. Tarantulasaurus
and
Manosaurs 3: Guru and Mahatma, Returns to Las Ventures

Printed in the United States
by Baker & Taylor Publisher Services